D1027293

Put A Spell on Me

NEW YORK TIMES & USA TODAY BESTSELLING AUTHOR

CYNTHIA EDEN

Dec 7 · 2021

This book is a work of fiction. Any similarities to real people, places, or events are not intentional and are purely the result of coincidence. The characters, places, and events in this story are fictional.

Published by Hocus Pocus Publishing, Inc.

Copyright © 2008, 2020 by Cindy Roussos

All rights reserved. This publication may not be reproduced, distributed, or transmitted in any form without the express written consent of the author except for the use of small quotes or excerpts used in book reviews.

Copy-editing by: J. R. T. Editing

A MESSAGE FROM CYNTHIA

PUT A SPELL ON ME was originally released in September 2008 as part of the EVERLASTING BAD BOYS anthology (back then, the novella had the title of SPELLBOUND). I've revised and updated the story, and now Luis is ready to take you on a sexy supernatural adventure. You're not afraid of monsters, are you? Because the creatures that hide in the dark aren't always bad. Sometimes, they're just…hot. Have fun and dive in!

CHAPTER ONE

She summoned him at midnight. The witching hour. Power swept through every inch of Serena Tyme's body, pulsing, growing, and the words of the spell poured from her lips, faster, faster.

Her arms shot above her head as the air crackled with magic. Thunder roared and lightning flashed across the cloudless night sky. Her eyes squeezed shut, just for one fearful moment, and when her lashes lifted, he was there.

The relief that rushed through her body had her trembling.

Then he spoke. "Nice body, sweetheart." His voice was deep and rumbling like the thunder. His golden eyes drifted over her skyclad form. Heat flared in the depths of his unusual eyes, then, voice slightly rougher, he demanded, "Now tell me who the hell you are and where the fuck I am."

Serena drew in a deep breath and watched the man's eyes dart to her chest. Jeez. Men. All alike—mortal or immortal—they always got distracted by a pair of breasts.

But she hadn't called him across space to ogle her. She crept forward and kept an anxious eye on him. She knew how much power he possessed, far more than a mere hereditary witch could hope to control. The sooner she explained things to him, the better.

After all, it wasn't an easy task to summon the devil. In fact, it took a damn lot of work to do that job.

The fire she'd built flared higher. Not her magic. His. Serena reached for her black robe, shrugged into it, and belted the robe quickly. *Good-bye, nakedness.*

"You didn't have to dress," he said. "I was enjoying the hell out of my surprise view." His powerful legs were braced apart as his arms rested easily at his sides. "But I am waiting on my answers."

His tone implied that he wasn't a happy waiting camper. She really hadn't expected him to be, though. She licked her lips, cleared a throat gone dry from chanting and the flames, and said, "M-my name's Serena Tyme. I'm a witch and —"

He grabbed her. Moved far too fast for her to follow, even with her slightly enhanced senses.

The circle she'd drawn should have held him in place, at least for a few minutes.

But it had failed.

Oh, damn. This was bad. Or, rather, *he* was bad. But, desperate times and all...

His hands had locked around her upper arms. A hold too tight to break, but not fierce enough to hurt, not yet. But the threat was in his steely grip and in the eyes that blazed down at her.

"I know you're a witch." The flames were reflected in his golden stare. A stare that burned brighter every moment. "No one else could have forced me here. Dammit, tell me—"

Her chin lifted. "Look, I'm answering your questions, okay?" He'd wanted to know who she was, and well, question one was now answered. As for the second question..."You're about an hour away from Atlanta, Georgia." When those eyes of his narrowed, she added, in a questioning tone, "In the U.S.?" The guy spoke with no accent, and she had no idea where he had been when her spell grabbed him. Although the where didn't really matter to her. All that mattered was that he stood before her now.

She saw a muscle flex along the hard, square line of his jaw. His black brows fell low as he studied her. His dark brows were a perfect match to the slightly too long, night-black hair that brushed the collar of his shirt. After a tense moment, he asked, "Why am I here, witch?"

Ah, this was the tricky part. She let her gaze dart down his body. He was dressed as any man would have been. Loosely buttoned black shirt. Jeans. Ragged boots. He looked normal. Could have been the guy next door.

If the guy next door happened to be the most powerful paranormal being in the Other world.

Because, despite what most folks thought, paranormals did exist. They lived right alongside humans. Demons, vampires, and witches like her—they were everywhere. But the humans, well, sometimes they had a hard time seeing what was right in front of them.

But she could see exactly who, or rather what, was in front of her.

The man before her had many names. After all, if the legends were true, he'd been roaming the world for centuries, and he'd continue to roam and fight and raise hell long after she was dust.

But the name most commonly given to him? Soul hunter. An eternal destroyer.

The rarest of the paranormals, soul hunters were produced from the mating of witches and all-powerful, level-ten demons—the true terrors of the demon world.

Soul hunters were gifted with the full powers of a hereditary witch, the full powers of a demon, and, as if they needed more of a dangerous bonus, soul hunters could live forever.

All the better to hunt.

She stared at him and couldn't contain the nervous tremble that shook her body. Hell, when she'd been a kid, her parents had told her that he was the boogeyman.

The immortal who came after the Other when they crossed that fine line between right and wrong. Because a soul hunter had more than just witch and demon powers. He was the immortal who could also steal a life away with but a simple touch.

"Always be good, Serena." Her mother's husky voice echoed in her mind. "Because the soul hunter, he comes after witches when they're bad."

Oh, yes, the threat of the big, eternal badass had kept her on the straight and narrow for years.

His fingers tightened around her arms. "Are you trying to piss me off?"

Serena blinked. "Uh, no. Really—I—" Oh, wait, what had he wanted to know? Jeez, she was tired. And scared. And so weak. The first binding had hurt her more than she realized. She'd barely managed to focus enough power for the summoning spell.

When his fingers moved, just a bit higher on her right arm, and he brushed the still tender flesh, she winced.

"Why. Did. You. Summon. Me." Gritted from between his clenched teeth.

Ah, right. Simple enough answer for that one. "Because I need you."

He glared down at her and she realized his features could have been handsome but they weren't—no, they were far too hard to make that "handsome" cut. His features looked as if they'd been carved from ancient stone. Too-sharp cheekbones, a nose that was too long, and a high brow. His skin was a darkened gold — made only more so by the flickering light of the flames.

As she stared at him, that hard mask slackened — just for a moment — and disbelief flashed across his face as he said, "You know what I am."

Of course. Would she have gone to the trouble of bartering for a dark spell if she hadn't?

"You know what I am, and you still summoned me." He shook his head as if he couldn't believe she'd actually called for him. "I bring death." He freed her. Stepped back. Clenched his hands into fists. "I'm not some kind of idiot demon that you can screw around with, sweetheart. I'm—"

"A soul hunter." *Soul eater.* That was the less-than-respectful term. Her voice was soft but firm as she continued, "I know. I also know that you're exactly what I need." The other witches in her coven had said that she was crazy. That she was courting the devil.

Summoning him didn't mean that she could control him, and soul hunters were extremely unpredictable.

In fact, until the menacing guy before her had appeared, she'd actually wondered if soul hunters were just myths. She'd never met anyone who'd known a soul hunter, and certain paranormals had sure been crossing that good/evil line at will lately.

Which brought up just why she needed her hunter.

"What is it that you need from me?" His words were a rumble of sound that seemed to shake through her body.

"I need you to save me." The mark on her arm burned with remembered pain. "And to do your freaking job and kill the bastard who is after me." Not just her, but her entire coven. If the soul hunter didn't help her, well, they'd all be dead soon. Serena was not ready to die. Not without putting up one hell of a fight, anyway.

Because she was one witch who wasn't about to burn easily.

CHAPTER TWO

Luis D'Amil shook his head and stared in disbelief at the shapely witch before him.

One moment, he'd been sitting in his favorite bar in Cozumel, and the next, he'd found himself in the middle of a forest and facing a naked woman.

A woman with a lot of power.

A woman who'd dressed far too quickly.

The witch had ripped him across time and space—hell, the least she could have done was let him look at those pink-tipped breasts a while longer. Would that have been asking too much? He didn't think so.

The witch had gorgeous breasts. It'd been far too long since he'd seen breasts that—

"Are you going to help me?" she demanded, and her voice held a tight, hard edge. *Serena.* He liked her name. It was somewhat musical. Soft.

Luis sighed and gave up the tempting image of her bare flesh. "No." He crossed his arms over his chest. "Now do your magic, and get me the hell out of here." He had a bottle of tequila waiting on him. He also had a demon he needed to hunt. Business waited.

Serena's mouth dropped open. Good lips, he couldn't help but notice. Sexy. Red and full. Just the way he liked them. Nice little heart-shaped face. Pretty. Cute nose, even if it did turn up a bit. High cheeks. Wide eyes. Green eyes. Cat eyes. Those eyes seemed to glow at him. And her hair...

Wild. A thick, curling black mass that skimmed her shoulders. The firelight burned brightly around them, making the red highlights lurking in the darkness of her hair flare to life. But even if the flames hadn't burned, he would have been able to see perfectly. It was the soul hunter's way.

Made the hunting easier.

His witch was all curves and soft skin. Not too thin—good, he'd never been attracted to a woman he couldn't hold tight. Lush breasts and round hips and sexy legs that—

"Didn't you hear me?" Serena nearly shrieked at him and Luis winced. "I said I need your help. Someone's after me—"

"Then go to the cops. The Other are everywhere these days. You'll be able to find a paranormal cop to help you."

"I don't trust cops."

"No, you don't trust human cops. Like I said, find a paranormal—"

"I don't trust any of them." Said with absolute certainly.

Ah, so his witch had experienced a bad run-in with the law, eh?

She exhaled, shaking her head. "Besides, no crime has been committed yet. Even if I went to them—and I'm not—what would I say? Someone's trying to bind me? Like they'd care!"

Someone's trying to bind me. Luis stiffened.

Witches were bound all the time. Some willingly because their powers were too much for them to handle. And some...not so willingly.

Long ago, the binding spell had only been used for protection. To bind those who would do harm. To stop the negative forces and to bind them safely. But the spell had been perverted by many over time, and the old ways were long gone.

"The cops can't help me." She glared at him. "Shit, isn't your job to catch the Other who go bad? To stop them from killing?"

Sometimes it was. Sometimes his job was just to clean up the blood left behind and make the humans forget the chaos they'd seen.

"Please." Her voice dropped, and for an instant, Luis swore he saw a flash of tears in her eyes. "I need you. My coven—someone's trying to destroy us."

He swallowed. Memories flooded through his mind. No, no, this couldn't be—

Serena pulled aside the top of her robe, baring her upper chest…the tempting swell of her breasts. Then she twisted and brought her right shoulder forward and he saw…

The first binding mark.

A long, angry red slash cut across the top of her arm. A slash that *hadn't* been made by a knife. It had been created by magic.

"It takes three to bind," she said, but he already knew that. His mother had been a very strong witch, and she'd taught him all the magic she knew, both light and dark. "Some sick bastard is out there. I don't know who he is or how he's doing this, but he's binding the members of my coven, one at a time."

A bound witch was a weak one. Perfect prey.

So very easy to kill.

Almost as easy as a human.

"Half of the coven fled when the first mark appeared on their flesh. I don't know how long the others will stay. They're scared, I'm scared, and I don't know what the hell to do."

She fixed her robe, tightened the belt, then closed the space he'd put between them. Serena reached for his arm. Her fingers felt so soft against him.

Her scent teased his nostrils. Roses. Lavender. A sweet, light blend. One that reminded him of innocence. Youth. A time long past for him.

Poor little witch. She thought the danger was hiding out there in the night, stalking her.

She didn't realize that the real threat was standing right in front of her. One touch, just one. If he focused his power, he could drain her dry in an instant. By the time she gathered the breath to scream, it would be too late.

Soul eater. Yes, he knew that was what many called him. Because he didn't just hunt. He took. Drained his prey dry until nothing was left but the shell of the body.

No soul. No power. No life.

Because he took everything.

"Three years ago, this same thing happened in LA." Her nails were long and sharp. Red. The hand that clasped him shook. "I wasn't in the coven that was marked, but my aunt—she was." Pain echoed in her voice and he saw the faintest quiver in her lips. "My aunt raised me, soul hunter. She took me in when my parents died." She shook her head. "I was eleven, she was seventeen—and she raised me, all those years, all by herself."

Her pain was deeper now.

"Then she got marked. I couldn't help her." Rage blended with the pain in her voice. "I couldn't help any of them. The witches in her coven were bound by a force they couldn't fight. Then one by one, they were killed."

His gut clenched. Hell, yeah, he knew about that case. He'd been fighting his ass off in Brazil at the time because a pack of panther shifters had laid a trap for him, and he'd been forced to eliminate them.

One shifter's soul after another.

"Some of the coven tried to run, but it didn't do them any good. They all still died." She drew in a ragged breath. "When the rest of the witches in LA found out, they were scared as hell. Most of them cut out of the city —"

"Like you did?" Why else would his little witch be all the way on the other side of the country?

"I couldn't stay in LA without Jayme. I couldn't live in her house, day after day, when she was gone." Serena shook her head, and a twisted smile curved her lips. "Besides, I thought I'd be safe here," she added softly. "And for a while, I was." Her lips, the ones that he really wanted to touch, firmed as her smile disappeared. "Then the asshole showed up here and started marking my coven — the only family I have anymore."

Ah, the coven. To hereditary witches, a coven tie was deeper than blood. The coven was power, security, trust. Life.

"You have to stop him." Serena's pointed little chin lifted into the air. "If you don't, then I'm dead."

He stirred at that, as a wave of tension rolled through him. Why should he care if one more witch — or even a dozen — passed to the next realm? There were others who would take her place.

And yet…

Her eyes. There was just something about them. So deep. Greener than the fields near his mother's old home.

Her eyes…innocence.

No. There was no way the witch was an innocent. Too much knowledge filled her voice, and she'd used the darkest of spells to rip him away from his promised drink.

"I will do anything," the witch said, and the desperation on her face and in her words was undeniable. "Anything, if you help me and my coven."

Ah, the pleading. He'd heard it before. Too many times to count. Normally, that shit didn't do a thing for him.

Her eyes. What was it about them? He searched her gaze and realized, no, that wasn't innocence in her stare. It was hope. How long had it been since he'd seen that? "There are thousands of other paranormals in this world who could use me," he told her, keeping his voice hard. His hands were fisted because he had the ridiculous urge to draw her close. "But I'm not a savior." He'd tried that route once and fucked up admirably. No, saving wasn't really his bit.

Seeking vengeance, sending monsters to hell—yeah, that was more his deal.

"Help me!" Her nails dug into his skin. For an instant, he imagined the two of them together. A dark room. Rumpled sheets. Her nails digging deeply into his flesh as she urged him on. "I have power, I can give you anything—"

Again with that magic word. *Anything*.

A dark, hungry temptation flickered through him. *Because I am my father's son*.

It had been far too long since he'd lain with a witch and tasted the magic on her tongue and sipped the power from her body.

Anything.

Those green eyes…

He lowered his head toward hers. She was so small, and her head barely came to his shoulders. She didn't back away when he closed that little bit of distance. Her eyes widened, but she held his stare. He could see the fire burning inside of her. He'd always liked to play with fire. "Are you trying to put me under a spell, witch?" A possibility. Her magic was more focused, even with the first binding mark, than any other witch he'd ever met. The hunger he was feeling, the stirring in his groin, it could be a trick.

Sure, a succubus was far better at laying a sensual trap than a witch, but with the right spell, Serena would still manage to turn him on.

Had managed to turn him on.

He'd been aroused from the first glimpse of her pale skin. As soon as the fog cleared and he'd seen her, he'd wanted to fuck her.

Not a usual response for him.

Killing, yes, that was normal.

But wanting to fuck on first sight, not so typical. Unless a spell was involved.

Serena licked her lips and the sight of her pink tongue nearly made him groan. "I-I only had enough power left to summon you. I can't hold a lust spell now."

He stared into her eyes and let his own power out. Truth. One of his handy talents. A soul hunter held the power of truth. He could hear lies. The words twisted and grated in his ears. He could discern truth with just a light push of power.

Before he killed, he liked to make certain he was executing the right monster.

He inhaled softly and caught her breath. Tasted her fear and her need. The witch would do anything to save herself and her coven. Luis realized he should probably admire that.

But he didn't.

Because the hunger he felt for her was growing too strong. His decision was made in that instant. A choice that came fast and wild, just like the need he felt for the sexy, little witch. "I'll find the one after you." It wouldn't be easy. The hunts never were. The psychotics were always smarter than they appeared, twisting and turning and leaving a tangled mess for him to sort out. "But it will cost you."

Hope flared even brighter in her gaze and her whole face seemed to light up. Not pretty. He'd been wrong on that. Beautiful.

Serena quickly began, "My coven will—"

"Not your coven, Serena." He wasn't interested in the others. No, he only cared about the witch who'd drained her powers to summon him, and then offered the man feared by all *anything*.

"What do you want?" Serena asked. There was no fear in her voice. Good, because he'd never wanted fear in his women.

"You."

She shook her head. "I don't understand." But the dawning realization was in her eyes, and her voice pitched too high in his mind. *Lie.*

Luis didn't call her on the falsehood. There would be time for that later. Just as there would be time for much, much more. "You will, witch. You will." Because he wasn't just talking about sex. A few hours of mindless pleasure. No, that would be far too simple.

He wanted all of her. Body and soul.

The hunt was on.

CHAPTER THREE

Exhaustion flooded Serena's body, but she walked doggedly forward, putting one foot in front of the other and focusing as hard as she could on not falling face-first onto the ground. She'd barely managed to cleanse the earth and break the remnants of her spell before the last of her power deserted her.

"Uh, is walking around naked out here a real good idea?" The soul hunter's voice rumbled from behind her.

She didn't stop. Couldn't, or she just might do that face-first routine she was trying so hard to avoid. "Look, hunter—"

"Luis." Soft. "Luis D'Amil."

Now she did pause, glancing over her shoulder. This was almost worth a fall. "Where are you from, Luis?"

"Once upon a time, I grew up in the area you know as Spain." His lips twisted into the faintest of smiles. "As the legends say, many of my kind hailed from that rich land."

Rich in magic. Always had been, but…"You don't sound Spanish." His voice was deep and dark, and completely devoid of any accent.

A shrug. "Witch, I've been everywhere on this planet. Languages, accents—after a few hundred years, they all blur."

"But you have to…live…somewhere now. I mean, you do have a house or an apartment or something, right?"

A shrug. "I travel. There are safe places for me to stay."

I travel. That was a big euphemism for stalking prey. She swallowed. "I didn't…ah…take you away from your family or anything, did I?" Serena hadn't even thought of that. *Oh, no.* What if he had a wife who was frantic because her hubby had up and vanished? But the guy had just propositioned her. Well, she was ninety percent sure he'd propositioned her, and the jerk had better not have a wife at home who—

His smile died. "I have no family left." Cold. No, arctic. Then, "My mother died in the Burning Times."

Oh, shit. The Burning Times. Those horror-filled years when witches had been hunted and hundreds, no thousands had been put to the flames. She shouldn't ask, really shouldn't, but…"Your father?" A level-ten demon was the only sire for a soul hunter, and level tens were all but immortal themselves.

In the demon world, there were several levels of power. The weaker demons were generally considered levels one through three — they barely had powers above a human's inherent psychic gifts. But the big, dangerous bastards who were ranked as level tens — well, those were the ones who could bring true meaning to the old phrase, "Hell on earth." Get them angry enough, and folks around the level tens would literally fry.

"My father died after her. He trusted me to save her. I didn't, and he couldn't live without her," he bit off the words. "See, witch, I'm not a savior — I couldn't spare my mother from the flames."

Her lips parted. *What do I say?* "I'm sorry, Luis." And she was. She knew just how much it hurt to lose a loved one to the fire.

He kept talking, as if he hadn't heard her — and maybe he hadn't. "I tried to save her. When I learned what the villagers had planned, I tried to help her. But I was too far away and couldn't get to her fast enough." His eyes narrowed. "And we all know just how fast witches burn, don't we?"

The image of her aunt's charred body flashed through her mind.

Serena swallowed back the bile that wanted to rise in her throat.

"Still sure you want my help, Serena?"

Taunting, but she could hear the echo of pain in his voice. Pain for the family he'd lost. Perhaps the soul hunter wasn't so very different from her after all. "Absolutely." He was her best bet. No, he was her only chance. "I'm sorry about your family, and you may not believe me, but I do understand."

The wind blew against her cheek. He stared into her eyes, and after a moment, his shoulders seemed to relax, just a bit. "I do believe you."

Well, that was something.

"But don't waste your time feeling sorry for me. I don't need your pity."

Her brows shot up. "Sympathy isn't the same thing as pity." *Jerk.*

"I need neither from you."

"And just what is it that you need?" Serena demanded, but she knew, dammit, deep down she knew —

The smile that curved his lips had her heart slamming into her chest — and her nipples tightening beneath the robe. *What in the hell is up with that?* Because, surely…she didn't think he was sexy. Did she? It wasn't like she was attracted to a *soul hunter*. No way. She wasn't that hard up. Was she?

Her heart drummed faster as her stare lingered on his smile. It was an oddly appealing, oddly sensual smile.

"I'll show you exactly what I need. Very soon." A dark promise.

Serena cleared her throat. *Enough.* Keeping her shoulders straight, she turned and resumed her march.

She felt his stare upon her with every step that she took. Heavy, hard and—

"You didn't answer me, little witch."

Answer him? What had the question been? She paused, and then, when the rest of his words sank in, she almost snorted. Little, her ass. Her abiding love for chocolate and all things dessert meant that she generally stayed out of the "little" category.

He snagged the back of her robe, and Serena stumbled, barely catching herself. She swatted back at him as she tried to get free. "Are you crazy? Let go! You don't just go around grabbing people!"

"Aren't you concerned about wandering around naked?" Luis demanded, and there was a different note in his voice. Anger?

Shoving a lock of hair out of her eye, she muttered, "Not really. This is coven land. No one but us should be out here." If any human intruders tried to cross the protected land, they'd find themselves turning and inexplicably walking the other way—fast.

Oh, but she did love the power of a good spell.

His hold on her loosened. "And we'll return to your house...with you unclothed?"

The guy was obsessed with her nudity. "I've got clothes in the car, all right?" She wasn't a flasher. Just a really desperate woman. Going skyclad had been a necessary component of the spell.

"Good." He finally released her.

"Glad you approve." Arrogant ass. But an arrogant ass that she needed.

They trudged the rest of the distance in blessed silence, and Serena soon saw the glorious sight of her beat-up Chevy and—

Luis grabbed her. His fingers locked around her wrist and he moved in a quick whirl to stand before her.

"What—"

"We're not alone." His shoulders were tight with tension.

As his response sank in, her eyes widened. But she hadn't sensed any danger. Even weakened, she should have felt a premonition of warning. Rising to stand on her toes, Serena peered over his shoulder. Then she saw them. Robed figures. Four. No, five of them. Walking from the woods near her car. Black hoods were drawn over their heads.

"Don't get in my way," Luis ordered. "I'll take them down. Stay back and—"

"No!" Perhaps her scream came too loudly.

But the hunter didn't even flinch.

She pushed against his back. "Luis, they're my coven!" What was left of the coven, anyway.

The women walked toward them. Serena scrambled to Luis's side as a nervous knot tightened in her stomach. One by one, the women drew back their hoods. First, Susan, the stylish matriarch who didn't look a day over fifty, but who Serena knew was actually pushing seventy. Patricia was next, her cloak falling away to reveal her long, straight black hair. Patricia's twin sister, Pamela, tossed back her hood almost in unison, exposing her delicate features and her close-cropped hair. Then Sasha, the youngest member of the coven, shoved back her covering. Sasha was barely nineteen, but, like Serena, she had grown up hard in a big city. The girl was tough as nails.

The last face to be revealed was that of Vanessa Donnelley, a fiery redhead Serena had met shortly after moving to the Atlanta area. Vanessa worked for Dr. Emily Drake—or, as the paranormals in the city called her, the Monster Doctor. The psychologist only treated the Other, and Serena was pretty certain that by the time this whole mess was finished, she'd have to pay the good doctor a visit.

Susan didn't look at Luis. Her horrified stare went straight to Serena. "What have you done, sister?" Her condemnation was clear to see.

Serena's chin notched up. "I'm trying to save this coven." They were all marked. They knew that death was coming. There was no sense in running or hiding. Why couldn't they see that?

"Is this him?" Sasha asked, eyes wide as she stared up at Luis.

Serena glanced to the left. Saw Luis smile. "What do you think, witch?" he murmured.

The women flinched.

"You've destroyed us," Susan whispered, but the words carried easily on the wind. "Soul hunters aren't to be trusted. You know that — you know the stories. They turned against the council years ago, slaughtered innocents — "

"Careful, lady, you're about to piss me off." Luis's words were easy, but the power suddenly pulsing in the air was hard.

Susan fell back a step. Hmm. Fell back, or was pushed? Before Serena could decide, the elder witch stiffened her shoulders and said, "He'll demand a price from you. From all of us."

Luis laughed. "Serena already knows my price, and she's agreed to pay." A shrug. "I have no interest in the rest of you."

Pity flashed across Susan's face. "What did you do, Serena?"

The only thing she could. Not like there had been a million options.

"I'm hunting now." From Luis. "I won't stop until I find the one after your coven."

"And then?" Vanessa's voice trembled. Normally she seemed so tough, but now, she was afraid. As they all were.

"Then I'll make him disappear," Luis replied. "Permanently."

Soul eater.

"We're leaving," Patricia announced quickly. "Getting out of town until —"

"Fleeing won't do you any good." Luis crossed his arms over his chest and stared down at her. "He's got your power trail, that's how he's binding you, all of you. He has something personal, and he can track you now, no matter where you go."

Yeah, Serena had been telling them all the same freaking thing. But when Luis said it, well, the witches gulped and whispered. And their plans changed. *Uh, hello, why didn't you listen to me?*

"Tell us when you find the bastard." Susan lifted her silvery mane proudly. "We will help you." The glow of magic lit her body.

Luis shook his head. "I don't need you to help me." He waved a mocking hand toward them. The witches were standing between them and Serena's car. "I just need you to get out of my way."

The witches moved, fast.

As Serena hurried toward her car, she was given one last warning.

"Be careful, Serena, once you use the dark magic, there's no going back." Susan's eyes flickered with power. She knew that the summoning spell Serena had used wasn't on the light spectrum. No, it tipped the scales sliding into the darkness—as did any spell that utilized force on the unwilling.

It wasn't like she'd *wanted* to go playing around with dark magic. Dark magic scared the shit out of her. When she'd been performing her spell, she'd heard the whispers of temptation from the damned. The lure of the ancient power.

But she'd resisted the whispers.

Serena had done her job—and gotten her soul hunter.

There had been no choice. She lifted her chin, squared her shoulders, and heard her mother's voice whispering through her mind, *"The soul hunter comes after witches when they're bad."*

Well, it looked like he was already after her.

But just what he planned to do with her...she was a bit afraid to find out.

***

His little witch needed more clothes. The black T-shirt and too-tight jeans barely covered her body, and Luis kept getting a teasing glimpse of the smooth flesh of her stomach.

The *tattooed* flesh of her stomach. A five-pointed star enclosed her navel, and a glittering gold hoop flashed from the center of her belly button.

Luis didn't even bother acting as if he weren't staring at her exposed skin. He'd been so busy admiring his witch's breasts earlier that he'd missed the tat and the piercing.

A pity, because the gold was sexy. Was she holding any more secrets on her body? He would discover them all — very soon.

She braked in front of a small ranch house. One on a perfectly normal-looking street. One that had small, blooming purple flowers along the sidewalk.

Her fingers clenched around the steering wheel. "I'm not going to just wait around while you hunt."

Her words had his brows rising.

After she unhooked her seatbelt, she turned to him with her jaw locked. "You're not gonna shut me out of this, do you hear me?" she asked. "I summoned you, and that means I have some control over you. You're not gonna shove me in some corner while you go off and hunt alone."

Ah. He almost smiled at her fierce words. Almost. Instead, he moved fast, catching her shoulders and pulling her against him. "Time for the rules here." Her lips were parted in surprise. It always amazed him that even the Other were surprised by the speed of his movements.

"Rules?" Her eyes were wide and filled with emotion. He could stare into her eyes for hours.

Luis drew in a deep breath and caught her scent. "Yeah, rules." Although, really, there weren't many. "First rule, no one controls me." Ever.

Her mouth opened ever more. "But —"

He kissed her. Took her mouth with his tongue and his lips like he'd been fantasizing about for the last half hour. And his witch tasted good. Sweet, hot. Fucking incredible. Her tongue moved against his, tentatively at first, as if she were almost afraid to respond.

He didn't want her fear.

His arms wrapped around her as he pulled her closer. Her breasts pushed against him and the feel of her nipples pressing into his chest made his dick surge to hard and eager attention. Luis stroked her with his tongue, holding on to his control, courting her, not demanding, but he needed her response.

Her willing response.

A moan built in the back of her throat. The sound shot straight to his cock and made the lust he felt for her double. Then her fingers were curling against him. Her nails dug into his shoulders.

And she kissed him with the same ravenous hunger that he felt.

Their mouths became rougher. Hands more demanding. The heat in the car ratcheted up about twenty degrees.

His fingers slipped down her arms. He wanted to touch her fucking perfect breasts. Touch them, lick them, suck them. He wanted to make her moan again for him. Over and over.

But Serena flinched, and he froze.

Not pain. From her, he didn't want pain or fear.

Only pleasure.

Slowly, he pulled back. Luis realized that he'd accidentally touched her binding mark. His finger stroked the flesh just under the jagged line. A silent apology. *I never want her in pain.*

Her breathing panted out, and so did his.

His gaze darted to the dark house behind her.

"Why did you kiss me?" Serena asked softly.

Luis blinked. Why? "Would have thought that was obvious."

"Sometimes I like for things to be spelled out."

Of course, the witch would like her spells. "Fine. I want you. Figured you could tell by the way I get hard just looking at you."

Her breath caught. "I…could not tell."

He wanted her mouth again. "You want me."

Her lower lip trembled. "You're cocky."

Wait, she wanted to talk about his cock—

"Fine, yes, I do. There's a whole weird attraction thing happening here that I did *not* expect."

Weird? Luis stiffened. "We are not humans. We don't have to pretend and play by their rules." The Other were highly sensual. Sex was pleasure. Sex was power. But did she think it was weird because… "Just what stories have you heard about me?"

"You're the boogeyman," she whispered. "You come for witches when they're bad."

Fuck, Serena. I would sure as hell like to come for you. Or, rather, with her. "Are you afraid of me?" He didn't want her fear. And he didn't want to hear her say that she feared him. "Forget that," he growled before he had the chance to hear her truth or lie. "I want you. You want me. Sex between us will be phenomenal."

"Is it...will you only help me for sex?"

Now Luis laughed. "I'm not that hard up." When she'd promised...*anything,* he hadn't been thinking about a fast screw in the dark.

He'd been thinking about forever. But they'd get to that, later. "Sex between us isn't about the deal we have. It's about me wanting you. You wanting me. Us going wild with pleasure. Because I can do that, sweet Serena." He brushed his lips over hers. Caught her lower lip in his teeth and gave a soft, careful bite. "I can make you wild." Once he had her safe and beneath him in a bed, he could make her go absolutely insane with pleasure.

A soul hunter guarantee.

CHAPTER FOUR

"What do you want from me?" Serena asked, and the sound of her husky voice was like a silken stroke right over his throbbing cock.

His answer? Everything — and that was what he would take.

"The summoning spell didn't give you any control over me." The minute he'd stepped out of her circle, her control had vanished. If she thought she'd be able to manipulate him, the lady was dead wrong. Best to get that cleared up right now.

Long ago, a council of Other elders had been created to keep the paranormal peace. They'd made the mistake of thinking they could control the soul hunters, too.

As far as Luis knew, no members of that illustrious council still lived. Not that he was particularly concerned with what had become of them all. Once he'd learned that the majority of those assholes had ignored their own so-called peace rules and slaughtered humans, he'd stopped caring about their lives.

And begun focusing more on their deaths. He'd hunted down several of the killers, despite their pretense of authority.

"My summoning spell brought you here." A satisfied smile curved her lips and drew him from the past. "That was what I wanted and —"

"No, what you wanted was to live." His words had her smile vanishing. "And I'll do my best to see that you do."

Before she could respond, there was a loud screech of sound, and something pounded against the windshield of her car.

Something small. Black. With claws.

Fuck.

He turned his head and glared out the windshield, meeting a pair of shining yellow eyes. "That damn well better not be your familiar."

Serena turned away and fumbled with the lock on the door. "He's not," she said. "Just a stray who wandered up a few days ago." She climbed hurriedly from the car and didn't bother glancing back at him.

His nostrils flared. The scent of her arousal carried easily to him. Like a shifter, he had very advanced senses. Smell, taste, sight, sound, and touch — they were all substantially heightened for him. Serena had been just as turned on by their encounter as he had been.

Good. That would make things easier.

When he got out of the car, Serena stood waiting near her small porch as she tapped one delicate foot. And the cat, a too-skinny, long-haired beast, had his tail wrapped around her legs.

She lifted her keys. "The poor thing looks like he's starving. I'm going to let him inside and find some milk or something for him."

The cat let out a satisfied purr.

Luis frowned.

His magic didn't work with animals. He wasn't a charmer and in all of his years, he'd never taken the soul of an animal-talker. Charmers generally weren't on the lists of fatal badasses who needed to be put out of their misery. Since he'd never taken one's power, that meant Luis couldn't communicate with beasts, but...

But he felt a whisper of dark power hanging around the cat.

Serena opened her door and the cat ran in front of her, tail up, and darted down the darkened hall as if he owned the place.

Serena stepped forward.

"Wait."

Her curls bobbed as she glanced back at him, and he could see the shadows of exhaustion under her eyes. His witch had been fighting a dark foe on her own for too many nights. But not any longer.

"I don't want you anywhere near that cat," he ordered.

A surprised laugh burst from her lips. "You can't be serious!"

But he was.

Brushing by her, and greedily inhaling her scent, he headed after the feline.

Behind him, Serena tapped a button, and the overhead lights flickered on.

The living room was to the left. Oversized couch. Cozy fireplace. Candles. Spell books.

And paint. Brushes. Easels. The heavy scent of the paint filled the air. So his witch was an artist. Interesting. And, judging by the paintings that sat on the two easels, she was very, very good.

A castle filled one canvas. Heavy grays. Dark blues. Intense reds and golds. A fortress under siege, battling the wind and rain and the night.

The second painting was of a woman. A portrait. A beauty with hair as black and curly as Serena's, but with green eyes that shone with light and happiness.

He hadn't seen happiness in his witch's eyes.

The cat nosed around the easel positioned near the window. Rubbed its fur against a brush that lay all but forgotten on the floor.

A personal item would be needed for the binding spell. Something Serena had touched. Something from her home.

He growled. The sound was a perfect match for a wolf, not a man.

The cat jerked his head up, arched his back, and hissed.

Luis bared his teeth.

The fur ball took off, running straight toward him, and Luis was ready. He grabbed the beast by the scruff of his neck and lifted him high into the air.

Yellow eyes blazed at him.

"Uh, what are you doing to the cat?" Serena cried out. "*Luis!*"

He didn't answer Serena. All of his attention was on the beast. Usually humans were the only ones who mistakenly thought animals were harmless. A witch should have known better.

"Tell your master I'm coming for him," Luis snarled, "and that he'd better start fucking running."

The cat's whiskers shivered. Then the feline twisted and fell from Luis's hands. He landed on all fours with a soft whisper of sound. The front door was still open, and he ran toward it, hissing.

Luis didn't bother chasing the animal. He had the creature's scent. The cat wouldn't get away from him.

After the cat hurtled out, Serena slammed the door shut and locked it. "I don't understand. I didn't sense evil from him—"

"He's linked with a charmer." Had to be. "The cat's been visiting you, probably all the coven, and providing the charmer with the link he needed to know you." A string, a piece of hair—the cat could have taken anything small back to his master. In order for a binding spell to work, a personal possession was needed. The cat had been a perfect thief.

She shook her head. "But charmers can't bind witches. They don't have that kind of power."

On that note, she was dead right. "The guy's not working alone." It was the conclusion Luis had reached as soon as he recognized the taint of power lingering around the cat. Which meant…"There's not just one bastard out there trying to take down your coven." No, not just one.

A smile lifted his lips. Ah, damn but he loved a challenge.

"We've got to go after them!" Serena cried out, looking both pissed and determined. "Let's go follow that cat and—"

"No."

Her mouth tightened. "I thought you were helping me."

"I am." He strode toward her. "You're dead on your feet. I'm getting you in bed."

Her breath jerked. "You're—no, you're just trying to go off on your own—"

He shook his head and touched her cheek. Such soft skin. So smooth. "I'm not going to leave you."

"I don't trust you."

Good. She shouldn't. Not ever. "You're tired. If you're going to hunt with me, you'll need your strength." It would take some time for her to recover from the summoning spell.

Her lips tilted in the start of a smile. "You're going to let me hunt with you?"

He'd never let another accompany him, but in the past, he'd gone to seek vengeance. Not to stop a crime from being committed. Since it was her life on the line, hunting with him seemed to be the least Serena deserved. So he nodded.

A relieved laugh burst from her lips. The sound was soft and sweet.

Nice.

Her beautiful smile stretched. "I thought you'd be pissed as hell at me for forcing you here, but you're —"

"I am." Pissed as hell. Yes, a fairly apt description.

The smile faded from her lips. "Oh."

"Don't forget who I am, not for a moment," he told her. She needed the warning, and he wouldn't give her another. "I agreed to help you, but I am most definitely pissed as hell at being yanked thousands of miles across the globe. You didn't have my consent, witch, and I don't take lightly to those who would seek to control me."

I summoned you, and that means I have some control over you.

Her words lay between them.

Serena swallowed and the soft click of sound seemed very loud. "Can you — can you truly kill with just a touch?"

His hand was on her cheek because he wanted to keep stroking her soft skin. Slowly, he trailed his fingers down the side of her face. Down the elegant column of her throat. His fingers curled around her neck. "Yes." One simple touch was all it took for him.

But he didn't have to give just pain and death with his touch. He could also give pleasure. He'd give that to her, when the time was right. And, once more, he found himself asking, "Are you afraid of me, Serena?"

Her eyes held his. So steady. So deep. "No."

Lie.

Her one whispered word grated in his mind. *Fuck.*

"Pity." He meant it. His hand rose slowly, cupping her cheek, and his head lowered toward hers. Her lips were parted. Almost as if she was waiting for his mouth. "Do you want me to kiss you again, witch?"

"Yes."

Truth.

His mouth took hers. Claimed it. Tasted the sweetness on her tongue and greedily took everything that her tender mouth had to offer. He'd have her naked soon. Beneath him in bed. Taking him deep inside of her.

Her body was supple against his. Her thighs shifted and he fought to control the impulse demanding that he reach down and search out all her secrets.

His tongue brushed over hers. Thrust into her mouth.

So good.

Her hands seemed to scorch his flesh. Even through the thin fabric of his shirt, he could feel the heat of her touch. If only they were naked, he'd feel her, everywhere.

Not now. This wasn't the right time. Not yet. She was too tired. Too weak.

Luis forced his head to lift. Serena's cheeks were flushed, her eyes sparkling, and her lips red and swollen from his mouth. "You want me." Luis said the words because he wanted no pretense between them. When he was between her thighs, thrusting as hard and deep as he could, he didn't want her pretending the sex was just some sort of sacrifice for the safety of her coven.

The price for the coven's protection would be met later.

The sex — that was just between them. A need he hadn't expected and certainly never imagined that he would feel for a witch who'd tried to control him.

He waited for her denial. None came.

The witch wasn't going to give him the speech about how she was a good girl. One who didn't sleep with strangers. With dangerous soul hunters...

No, she wasn't giving him that speech. Because good witches didn't use dark magic.

"That's what you want from me, then?" Serena finally asked him. "My body?" Still so calm. Too calm.

"I'm going to be taking a lot more than just your sexy body, Serena." She'd learn what he wanted soon enough. "Besides, don't you want me?" If there was anything he'd learned about witches, it was that they were sensual creatures. It was partly due to the magic that constantly streamed through their bodies. All of that glorious, rich power.

Sex was necessary for witches. Not as necessary as it was for sex demons, but witches mated often. With Serena's power running low, she'd need the brief boost she'd get from a hard climax of pleasure.

And the thing about witches...they had a reputation for always leaving their lovers well satisfied.

A succubus usually only cared about her own pleasure.

A witch was different. Shared pleasure made a witch stronger.

"You know I want you." Her words came slowly.

Truth.

"I shouldn't," she added, and her breath feathered over his face. "It's the wrong time and you're sure as hell the wrong man."

His brows shot up. Well, well, she wasn't pulling her punches. Something he liked.

"If I wanted to play with a devil, there are any number of demons I could find in this town for a fix."

A growl worked in his throat. He didn't want to think of Serena with another. Not when he hadn't even come close to possessing her yet. "No one else," he ordered and meant it. The lust between them was unexpected as hell, but Luis had never been the sharing type. He'd have Serena, and no being — human or Other — would touch her while he was near.

"And no one else for you," she shot back, and her words held the same edge of possession that his had.

"Agreed." Luis's response was instantaneous. He wanted no other. Once more, he let his hand move to her throat. His fingers slid over her neck. Beneath his touch, he felt her pulse beating far too fast.

Serena's hunger matched his, but her strength didn't.

Not now.

"I won't hunt without you," he told her again. Then, "Don't be afraid…"

Her eyes widened. "What? Why are you —"

"I'll be here when you wake."

Understanding dawned too late in her gaze.

Exhaling slowly, he blew a stream of magic right at her. She sagged against him. Her body went limp as sleep claimed her. Luis pulled her close.

And thought about the magnificent twists of fate.

And how very, very easy it was to kill a witch.

***

"Anubis."

The black cat hissed and arched his back as Julian Kathers crouched before him. Julian listened intently to the news. A frown pulled at his brows as anger churned within him. "Dammit."

The warlock who sat on the other side of the room arched a brow. "Trouble, charmer?"

Julian stroked the cat's back. He was trying his best to calm Anubis. The cat was shaking. Scared to death. With good reason. "A soul hunter is in town."

For the first time in the fifteen years that Julian had known the warlock, fear flickered over Michael Deveaux's face. "Bullshit."

Anubis hissed again.

"He's with one of the witches," Julian added. Fucking bad news. The witches were easy enough to pick off one at a time, after they'd been bound, anyway. And he sure did enjoy the sight of a witch bitch burning, but—

But the soul hunters were a different matter. He'd never gone up against one of them. Didn't have the power to face one.

Did the warlock? Julian's heart pumped fast at the thought. Maybe. *Maybe.* A wild laugh sprang to his lips, but he bit it back. *I'd love to see a soul hunter die.*

Maybe the bastard would beg. Plead. Julian loved it when prey pleaded. The pitiful pleas made death so much sweeter.

Fuck, but he should have been born stronger! Not as a worthless charmer who could only talk to strays. Those witch bitches in his old neighborhood had taunted him and used their magic to make every day of his life miserable, one spell after another.

But he'd shown them. He'd shown them all.

A witch's screams were so sweet, and the flesh of a witch smelled so very good when it burned. The laugh he couldn't hold back any longer broke from his lips.

The warlock had swiped a hell of a lot of energy from the witches over the years. Yes, maybe he could do it—

Another laugh escaped from Julian. The cat shook beneath his petting hand.

The warlock rose, and the light of a nearby lamp reflected for a moment in his blond hair.

"The hunter saw the cat?" Michael's voice was calm, even.

No fear—of course not. Because he knew that he could take the soul hunter.

Excitement had Julian's heart drumming even faster.

Anubis arched his back again and his whiskers twitched.

"Yes, the hunter was with the witch—the black-haired one, Serena—at her house. He followed the cat inside."

Anubis meowed. A high, plaintive sound.

Michael tensed. "What did the damn cat just say?" What could have been anger flared in his voice as he stalked forward.

Julian wasn't laughing any longer. "The soul hunter wanted a message delivered. He said he'd be coming." *And that I'd better start fucking running.*

But Julian hadn't run from anyone, not since he was sixteen and those witches at his school had thought it would be funny to chase him after class with one of the stone gargoyles that should have forever stayed resting on the roof of the old building next to his high school.

They'd known he was Other, so they'd felt confident in playing with him. The witches never would have worked tricks like that on humans.

For the longest time, he'd heard their laughter when he closed his eyes at night.

Then, after he'd hooked up with the warlock, he'd been able to hear only their screams.

"He'll have the cat's scent." The momentary heat that had entered Michael's voice was gone. He walked around Julian. He kept a careful distance from Anubis.

Michael had never liked his cat, Julian knew that. But he'd sure used Anubis every chance he got. Such a perfect pet. So good at sneaking into the homes of witches.

Witches always had a soft spot for black cats. Fools.

"We can be ready for him," Julian said. Confidence and the thrill of the upcoming kill filled him. "Let the hunter come, we'll gut him and—"

Snap. Julian's words ended. His hand stopped stroking the cat.

***

Slowly, the warlock lifted his hands from Julian's neck.

So easy to kill charmers, Michael thought. Almost as easy as killing humans. The best part? He hadn't even needed to waste a drop of his magic.

"One problem down," Michael muttered and smiled at the cat. The soul hunter could trace the cat's scent all he liked now, and he'd just find death waiting for him.

Lifting his hand, Michael motioned for the cat. "Here, little kitty…come to me…so I can send you to hell with your master…"

The cat turned and ran. Anubis jumped onto the window ledge and then dove into the night.

Michael laughed. The cat had been smarter than the charmer. Not really surprising.

So, the witch, Serena, had summoned a soul hunter. Interesting. Resourceful. Usually the witches just ran and hid when the first binding mark appeared on their flesh. Hmm. Serena had to be strong. Most of her kind couldn't use a summoning spell even at full power, much less initially bound.

She's not your average witch. Good. It had been far too long since he'd taken a strong witch's magic.

He stepped over Julian's body. Headed for the door. He'd face the soul hunter when he was good and ready…and at a place of his choosing. But first, first he had to finish the witches. He'd need every last drop of their power to kill the soul hunter on his trail.

Fortunately, he knew just which of the coven members he would mark for first death.

The lovely Serena.

CHAPTER FIVE

She woke to find him standing at the foot of her bed. Dawn had yet to creep across the sky, so he stood, cloaked in the shadows and darkness. His golden eyes glittered at her. There was no mistaking the dark hunger in his stare.

Lust.

Well, hello to you, too. Serena sat up slowly. She was still dressed, just missing shoes, and a sheet had been pulled over her body. She licked her lips as she stared up at him and tried to figure out her next move. The silence in the room was thick and heavy and she waited…

Luis crept around the bed. The carpet muffled the sounds of his footsteps. Closer, closer.

Her heart hitched faster, but she didn't speak, not yet.

He neared the side of her bed. Stopped and gazed down at her with his burning eyes. So much need. Was the same desire reflected in her own stare? She had *not* expected the attraction between them. Who expected to meet a soul hunter and get turned on? That didn't usually happen, or at least, she'd sure never heard about it before. He wasn't supposed to have the allure of an incubus, but every time she was near Luis, Serena...ached. Wanted. She'd even been dreaming about him. About having his hands on her body. His mouth. When she'd woken and he'd been standing there...

I want him.

It had been so long since she'd been with a lover. So long since she'd let down the wall around her and trusted another to be close to her.

You can't trust Luis, a soft, niggling voice warned.

No, she couldn't. She shouldn't.

But she did want him. And that was a problem.

Her last lover had left over a year ago. Gotten tired of her secrets. A human, he'd sensed she was holding back on him, but Serena had never felt ready to tell James the truth about herself. She'd been afraid he would run from her. Then, one day, she'd come home to find a note waiting for her.

And no James.

He ran even without knowing the truth.

After a few days, she'd stopped missing him.

Would the same thing happen when her hunter left? When his job was done, would she be able to write him off as easily?

When Luis's hand brushed over her cheek, she jumped.

"I want you." His voice, so deep, almost guttural, growled from the darkness.

Just the sound of his voice, hardened with hunger, had her nipples tightening. *Jeez, eager much?*

She'd never been with a man as supernaturally strong as he was. Her lovers had generally been mortals, except for the bear charmer and the fox shifter, and—

"Say no, and I will leave the room. Right now."

"I'm not saying no." She wasn't going to lie to him or herself. "I don't know how I can want you so much." So soon. "It…scares me."

"You don't need to be afraid of me."

"I thought everyone was supposed to fear the soul hunters."

His fingers skimmed along her jawline. "You're not everyone."

Her heart seemed to warm. "You knocked me out, didn't you?" Used a spell on her. He'd done something to make her sleep.

"You were dead on your feet. You were only staying awake because you didn't want me to think you were weak. You needn't worry about that. I know you're one of the strongest beings I've ever met."

Really? Her shoulders straightened. "Flattery is great, but you don't get to use some mojo on me—"

"All I did was push you to do what *you* wanted." A pause. "I won't do it again. I just…you were exhausted. You needed to rest. I wanted to help." His stare held hers. "I'm kinda rusty at that."

"I noticed." She also noticed that he was still touching her, and she was liking his touch way too much. She was leaning into his touch because she liked it so much. She wanted *more* of it.

And Serena could tell by the hungry look in his eyes that he knew exactly how she felt. "Luis…"

"You want me. I want you. You know that you need the pleasure we can give each other."

Pleasure was power in their world.

"Don't think about anything else right now…nothing but me." His hand curved under her chin. Tipped back her head and—

He kissed her. Pushed his tongue past her lips and took her mouth just as he'd done before. And, just as before, her blood began to heat, desire to uncoil, hard and fast, within her. Her hands caught his shoulders. She held on tight.

Magic.

Passion.

Power.

It was all there in his kiss, and she wanted it—wanted him. For the first time in twenty-nine years, she decided to take what she wanted. Screw the consequences. She'd never been the one-night-stand type. Still wasn't. But this was different. He was different. This was about sex and power. Magic. This was about—

It's about the way I feel when he's near. Like all control is gone and I just want to take.

Serena's lips parted more, and she met him, tongue to tongue, mouth to mouth, kissing greedily, rising to hold him tighter.

Fuck being the pristine one. Holding out for love—that had never worked so well for her.

Going for the wild, mad ride of pleasure— she'd see how that worked out instead. Besides, death was on her trail, and she wanted to make certain she lived as much as she could. Every. Single. Moment.

"I need you," Luis rasped the words against her mouth.

Her lashes lifted and she found Luis staring down at her. A rush of sensual power flooded through her veins and Serena heard herself respond, in a voice gone husky with matching desire, "Then why don't you take me?" Holy hell, had she just said that? Out loud? Since when was she all tempty? She didn't normally have the confidence for that kind of—

In the next second, she was flat on her back in the bed. Luis was over her. Her hands were pinned in the bedding. His legs tangled with hers. The thick length of his cock pushed against her.

Yes.

This was what she wanted. Wild. Fast. Hot. Hard. No over thinking. No hesitating. Just sex. Magic. Power.

His mouth blazed a path down her neck. Lips branding. Tongue licking. And his teeth…

Serena shuddered when the edge of his teeth grazed her flesh. Need poured through her. She twisted beneath him. She wanted to feel his naked skin against hers. "There are too many clothes in the way!" The words tumbled from her lips as she drew in ragged breaths.

He freed her hands as he reared back. His long, strong fingers caught the edge of her shirt. Jerked it over her head. The garment disappeared, tossed somewhere in the room — she had no idea where and didn't care.

She'd put on a bra when she'd dressed back at her car. Now he made quick work of ditching her bra. He unhooked it, and the lacy cups fell aside.

My turn. Her hands found his shirt front, jerked it open and sent buttons flying across the bed.

His hands cupped her breasts. Teased. Fingertips caught her nipples, caressed, then his dark head lowered. The warm, wet lap of his tongue sent a shock wave through her. "Luis!" Her nails skated down his chest. Power was in the air around them. Energy vibrated against her skin.

For a witch, there was magic in sex. The renewing power of life, and the blissful wonder of pleasure. Just what she needed.

No, *he* was what she needed.

He licked her nipple. Sucked. Used the faint edge of his teeth in a sensual bite. A moan escaped from Serena as she arched her hips and rubbed against the hard — and long — length of his cock.

Flesh to flesh. That was how she wanted him — and how she would have him.

Her hands gripped his upper arms. Tested the muscles, then caressed his chest as her hands began to trail down his body. His strong abs rippled beneath her fingertips. The man was like some kind of perfect freaking statue.

Not a man.

More.

He licked her nipple once more, then lifted his head. "Serena…"

Such hunger. Raw lust. She loved the way he said her name.

Her fingers caught the top of his jeans. Unhooked the button and eased down the zipper with fingers that shook with eagerness.

"Are you still afraid of me?" Luis asked and his voice was as demanding as the hands that were stroking her body.

"No." Right then, she couldn't get close enough to him. Afraid? Only that he'd stop.

Her vision wasn't shifter strong, but she caught a glimpse of his smile, the flash of his teeth as he rumbled, "Good answer." His hand slipped down her stomach, hesitated over her belly button. "I want to kiss you."

Hadn't he already? What—

He shifted his body, pulling back and bringing a cry of protest to her lips. *Do not stop!*

But he wasn't stopping. She didn't have to worry. His mouth pressed against her stomach. His fingers eased open the top of her jeans, and he licked her. A long, slow lick right along her belly—and along the piercing she'd gotten as a birthday present just last year.

Her heels dug into the mattress and her thighs clenched around him. "Get rid of the jeans," she ordered. Serena meant hers *and* his. She'd never been one for too much foreplay. She loved the act of sex too much. The slide of bodies. The hard thrusts. The joining.

She wanted to join with Luis. To mate.

A growl shook his body and an answering moan rose in her throat. When his fingers pushed the denim completely off her hips and his breath fanned over the front of her panties, she arched toward him, ready—

Sudden, white-hot pain lanced her—burning, cutting into her upper arm. The agony was so intense that she contorted as tears trickled down her cheeks.

Luis immediately froze. "Serena?"

She clenched her teeth and tried to choke down the pain. It felt as if someone were cutting her arm. Driving a knife all the way to the bone and carving her flesh.

Not again. Goddess, no, not the second mark.

"Fuck!" The cry was Luis's. He jerked away from her and shot from the bed. She heard his deep voice chanting a spell of protection because he'd obviously realized what was happening to her.

But his spell would do no good.

The lights flashed on in her room. A burst of air tousled her hair. The pain began to recede. Throbbing now, in time with the rapid beats of her heart. She squeezed her eyes shut. She wanted to block out the light. And she didn't want to look at her arm.

Because she knew exactly what she'd see.

A second binding mark meant her powers would be even more limited. Who was doing this to her?

A feather-light touch upon her shoulder had her screaming even as her eyes snapped open.

Luis gazed solemnly at her. His expression appeared so fierce—as fierce and deadly as he'd looked when she'd first summoned him.

"Are you all right?" he asked softly.

No. She was most definitely not all right. Her life was spiraling out of her control. Some sick bastards were screwing with her and her coven, and a second binding mark meant her time was running far too low.

"When did the first mark appear?" Luis pushed.

Serena pulled in a slow breath. The passion she'd felt so deeply moments before was gone. It had been erased by a tide of pain. And rage.

"When the Blood Moon took the night." Had it really been just a few nights before when the full moon had risen so powerfully into the sky? And the first mark had appeared.

Steeling herself, Serena finally dropped her gaze to stare at the flesh of her upper arm. Already, the binding cut looked like a scar. Four inches long. The flesh was raised. Angry red.

Only one more mark to go, then the spell would be complete. She would be as helpless as a human.

Luis's fingers hovered over the mark as if he wanted to touch her, but was afraid.

"It's a warlock, you know," Luis said.

Serena's gaze was on her arm. "I know." The throbbing continued. The aching flesh pulsed as she stared at the skin. A warlock.

In the Other world, those who practiced their power in good faith—following the rule to harm none, were termed witches or wizards.

But a witch who crossed that line, or a wizard who harmed innocents, well, then that person was given a new designation.

Warlock.

Shunned by the coven. Expelled from the magical community.

Alone to work the dark magic.

She'd known, of course, for only another witch would be able to work a binding spell. Demons didn't have the power. A djinn couldn't strip a witch of her magic.

No, it took one of her own to work spells like this.

A fact that made the betrayal all the harder to handle. Not that betrayal was ever particularly easy to handle, but...

His fingers brushed over the marks. She sucked in a sharp breath because Serena expected the burning pain to flare to life again except —

Except it didn't. She felt a cool balm on her skin. The throbbing eased. The redness lightened.

Her eyes widened.

His head bent toward her, and he pressed a kiss to the second wound, then the first.

The pain vanished completely.

Serena stared at him, stunned. He was the bringer of death, not a healer. "How did you do that?"

He looked up at her through his lashes. His mouth poised over her arm.

A spark of remembered need had her shifting and realizing that she was mostly nude and that if she'd had just a few minutes more before that bastard had struck —

Well, she wouldn't have been thinking about pain.

"I don't just bring fear and terror." Another kiss, then he eased away. "I can also soothe pain or..." His gaze dropped to her breasts. "Give pleasure."

Oh, yes, she'd gotten a firsthand sample of that pleasure. And she wanted more. Serena swallowed and yanked on her bra. She'd love to just lie back with Luis and get a few more samples, but..."W-we've got to go after them." The warlock and his charmer. "If the warlock marked me, he could be trying to mark the others—we have to go!"

Luis gave a grim nod but asked, "Are you certain you're up to facing him?"

Like she was going to back down. "This is my life he's screwing with so, yes, I'm definitely ready."

"Then we'll fight now." Again, a dark heat flashed in his eyes. "And later..."

We'll fuck.

Yes, they both knew exactly what would happen later.

***

Damn. Damn. Damn. He was going to make the bastard pay. He'd hunt him down, no, hunt *them* down, and make them beg for mercy.

Then he'd kill them.

Luis knew he was after a team of killers. Had to be a charmer working with a warlock. There was no way that the charmer who controlled the black cat would be able to bind the witches on his own.

The memory of Serena's pain-filled cry echoed in his mind. His hands clenched and magic snapped in the air around him.

Oh, yes, those bastards would pay in blood.

He'd been seconds away from claiming Serena, then some assholes had fucked up his plans and hurt his witch.

Luis couldn't wait for the fighting to begin. He was definitely in the mood to kick ass and send a few deserving paranormals straight to the next world. *The sooner, the better.*

"Stop!" He gave the order when Serena's car turned the corner of Ruther's Lane.

The window on his side of the car was down. He'd been following the trail of the black cat—using his enhanced sense of smell to catch the feline's scent. He'd also been tracking the taint of the dark magic that had hung heavily on the cat—a taint that, to his eyes, appeared as a fine mist in the air. A mist that led him straight to the small shop at the end of Ruther's Lane.

"Turn off the car," he directed, his tone quiet.

Serena obeyed instantly. "Is this—is the warlock here?"

He wasn't sure, but the cat had been there. The cat had gone inside the antique shop that boasted the sign, HIDDEN TREASURES.

Dawn had come. The sun had eased up into the sky and chased away the shadows. They were on a small business street, one lined with curiosity shops and galleries. One that would soon be teeming with humans.

Hmmm. Those humans could be a problem. Luis knew he and Serena would have to move fast. Luis turned to Serena, "Let's—"

She shoved open her door and hopped outside.

He blinked. Obviously, his witch was ready to kick ass, too. He could respect that.

She'd changed her clothes before they left. Slipped on a long blouse that covered her arms and her binding marks. She wore jeans that hugged the rounded curves of her hips and thighs. Her small feet were encased in snug, black leather boots.

Serena had even managed to find him a shirt, a fact that pissed him off. Why the hell would his witch have men's clothes handy? And she hadn't conjured them—a whole assortment of men's shirts had been hanging in the back of her closet. She'd muttered something about her ex leaving the items behind. The bastard had better not be coming back to claim the clothes—or Serena.

Luis climbed from the car and glanced around to make certain no human was nearby.

The last thing he needed was a nosy mortal catching sight of his battle. Or of him.

Satisfied that the humans hadn't yet come to play, his hand lifted, and he pointed toward HIDDEN TREASURES. The shop's windows were dark, and a CLOSED sign hung haphazardly against the front door.

His nostrils twitched as he caught a darker, pungent smell on the wind.

Hell. That scent wasn't a good sign.

"Luis?" Serena called his name softly.

"Death's waiting, sweetheart." No mistaking that dank scent. "Stay on your guard."

She gave a slow nod. Her delicate shoulders squared.

And Luis led the way toward the scent he knew too well.

CHAPTER SIX

The door was locked, but one quick jerk of his hand made the cheap lock shatter. Luis shoved open the door and heard the squeal of an alarm. His gaze darted around the room and immediately locked on the small black box with the blinking red dot.

Luis grabbed a nearby silver candlestick and threw it. The heavy candlestick hurtled end over end toward the alarm. When it smashed into the box, blessed silence filled the air. So much for going in quietly, but then he'd never really been the quiet type.

Besides, for one of the bastards he was chasing, the noise wouldn't matter. After all, not much could wake the dead.

"The cops will be coming," Serena said, and there was no missing the worry in her soft voice. Cautious witch. "Because of the alarm, the security service will alert them—"

"Then we'd better move quickly."

A hiss sounded from the back of the store. An all too familiar sound. Damn cat. Luis hurried forward and saw the small beast pacing in front of an old, scarred door.

The cat arched his back at Luis's approach and bared his teeth.

"Out of the way." Not in the mood to deal with the feline, Luis flashed his own teeth.

The cat turned and ran back toward the entrance of the shop.

"Ah, Luis..." Serena stood behind him. So close he could feel the warmth of her body. "Was that cat *guarding* this door?"

"It sure looked that way." He lifted his hand and touched the door. Then Luis sent the entire door crashing to the floor with one hard punch. Sometimes enhanced strength could be a real bonus. He saw the tangle of bright red hair first. Then his gaze darted along the body. *Not moving.* The bastard's neck was twisted, and his horrified eyes were wide open.

The SOB didn't have any defensive wounds that Luis could see. Didn't look as if he'd put up any fight. Probably never saw death coming.

Because he'd trusted his killer?

Serena sucked in a sharp breath. "Oh, goddess, is he a human?"

"No." A quick scan showed that no one else was in the small room. Luis crouched beside the body. He reached out his hand—

"Meow." The black cat ran back into the room and pressed against the dead man's side.

Luis exhaled. "It's the charmer." The asshole who'd been working with the warlock. *Dammit. The kill should have been mine.*

"I don't understand."

He glanced up at her. Serena's face had gone pale, and her eyes were staring fixedly at the body. No, at the bastard's twisted neck. Hell, Serena looked ready to faint.

"W-why is he dead? If he was working with the warlock—"

The cat's head prodded the charmer's side as he tried to get his master to wake.

"Not gonna happen, buddy. Might as well give up on that shit," Luis muttered to the small creature and rose to his feet. Then he lifted a brow and explained to Serena, "The charmer is dead because the warlock knew I could trace the cat back to his master."

Her gaze jerked away from the body. Understanding dawned on her face. "Once you had the charmer, you could have tracked the warlock."

Yep. That had been his plan. As easy as connecting the dots.

Or, it should have been that easy. But the warlock had decided to cover his ass and throw a dead body in their path. How annoying.

Serena swallowed and lifted her hand to her throat. She even swayed a little bit. Not a good sign.

"Uh, is this your first body, Serena?" How many corpses had he seen in his time? Hundreds? Thousands? The sight of the dead no longer fazed him. But Serena was another matter.

"Not my first." Her brows pulled low. "My aunt — I found what was left of her."

The urge to go to Serena — to hold her — rocked through him. Whoa. What the hell was up with that? He was not the comforting type.

The killing type. The fucking type, sure.

Not comforting. Never that. The witch was screwing with his head.

Luis found himself taking a step forward and actually blocking her view of the dead body. "Nothing can be done for the bastard now," he told her gruffly. *Why am I trying to shield her? What. The. Fuck?*

In the distance, a siren wailed.

Serena shook her head, and some of the color seemed to return to her cheeks. Her gaze darted around the room. "We've got to get out of here," she mumbled. "We've got to — " She broke off. Her eyes widened and then she ran across the small room. Her hip thumped against the side of a desk as she skidded to a halt.

"Serena?"

"This is Vanessa's." She lifted a long, blue hair ribbon. "She had it in her hair last week." Her fingers reached for a swatch of fabric. "And Susan was working on a quilt just like this — no!

Dammit!" She dropped the fabric. "The bastard has us all right here!"

Actually, Luis knew the warlock had to have even more of their belongings stashed somewhere else. In order to continue the spell, he'd need to hold one personal article from each witch. No way would the guy have left all his treasures behind.

The wails of the sirens were getting closer.

Serena swore, then started to frantically grab all the witches' possessions.

He frowned at her. "What are you doing? We don't have time—"

"And what if the cops connect any of this stuff to the coven? We'll be screwed!"

She was right. So he started helping her, fast. Their hands were overflowing when they ran from the store. Probably looked as if they were robbing the place. Fate was on his side, for once, though, because the street was still deserted. Good. He wouldn't have to waste any magic on the humans.

They hurried to the waiting car, tossed the materials inside and—

A police cruiser hurtled around the corner. Brakes screeched and the lights above the vehicle flashed in a blur. Two officers jumped out, and the men had their guns drawn. "Freeze!" The command came in unison.

Serena stilled near the driver's side door of her car. "Um, officers," Serena began nervously, "this isn't what you think—"

"We're not here," Luis interrupted. His voice carried easily as he walked toward the cops. He called up the power he'd been given by his father and focused on the two men with guns.

His father had been a level-ten demon. Tens were the strongest of the demons and those who could most easily control the minds of humans.

As Luis advanced, the guns lifted higher. The cops' hands shook. "D-don't m-move." The shaky order came from the guy on the right, the one who looked like he was barely twenty-one.

"Luis." Horror shook Serena's voice.

Horror because Luis knew she was used to living in her safe coven world, a world where the good rules said not to hurt humans. Well, she didn't need to worry. Luis wasn't going to hurt these two, unless that option became absolutely necessary.

He really did try to spare the innocents when he could. It was those who deserved his fury that he unleashed his power upon. And then Luis let the fire rage.

But he *would* make the human police officers forget. He'd use a hard compulsion to drive the memory of him and Serena forever from their minds.

"You didn't see us," Luis told the men softly, as Serena waited tensely behind him. "When you arrived on the scene, there were no other cars in the vicinity."

The young kid's eyes bulged. He swallowed, once, twice, then his gaze darted to Serena, and his gun moved to aim straight at her chest.

"Drop the weapons!" Luis snarled. His heart lurched as something he'd not felt in centuries reared its head.

Fear.

Fuck.

Both guns hit the ground with a clatter.

Luis turned his head and glared at Serena.

She blinked. "What?" Then she looked over her shoulder, as if expecting to see some kind of threat.

She was the threat. A threat to him. Hellfire. Serena was the danger his mother had warned him about so many times. A weakness.

Luis ground his back teeth together. This wouldn't do. Not at damn all. With an effort, Luis turned his attention back to the cops. "You didn't see us," he repeated, forcing the compulsion deeper. The kid was stronger than the slightly balding fellow behind him. Could be the rookie even had a touch of psychic power.

But there was no way either of the humans were strong enough to resist him.

Another paranormal could fight his power because the Other could resist Luis's compulsion. Serena would be able to resist because of her witch blood.

But the humans before him didn't stand a chance of fighting him.

"Get in the car," he told Serena, not wanting to push his luck. He didn't want to risk a shifter or charmer cop pulling up on the scene. They needed to get out of there without any other trouble.

But she didn't move.

Oh, by the grave of — *"Serena,"* he growled as his gaze snapped to her. *"Why aren't you jumping in the freaking car?"*

"The cat," she said and bit her lip. "We can't just…leave him alone with that dead body."

His eyes closed for a moment. Witches and their soft spots for animals. Had to be a leftover trait from their heavy familiar days. "Fine," he snapped out, but he was not happy with the situation. Not even a little bit. Who would be happy with this shit?

Luis jabbed his index finger in the rookie's direction. "There's a cat inside. A furry, skinny-as-hell stray."

The officer waited.

"He's yours now."

The rookie nodded.

"Satisfied?" Luis threw the question at Serena as he hurried around the car. More sirens were crying in the distance, probably because he'd heard someone from the station trying to contact the officers on their radio during his compulsion, and the men hadn't responded as requested.

"For now," Serena allowed as she slid into the car. A moment later, she revved the engine. Then Serena threw the car into reverse and shot backward, narrowly avoiding a hard slam into the side of the police cruiser. She shifted gears, twisted the car into a tight turn, and floored the gas as she roared down the road.

A touch of admiration filled Luis as she got them out of the about-to-be-swarmed neighborhood in less than thirty seconds.

Nice.

His witch had secret talents. Or just mad, bad driving skills.

"Are you, Luis?" Her voice floated to him.

His gaze whipped to her face. Locked on her profile. "Am I what?" Had he missed something?

"Are you satisfied?" she asked.

The flash of fear he'd felt moments before returned. No, he was far from satisfied. She was too vulnerable. The human cop could have shot her. Could have killed her.

And Luis had just found her.

"Fuck, no," he snarled, and her gaze flew to his. He leaned closer to her. Luis curled his fingers around her right thigh. "I'm not even close to satisfied." *But I will be.* His fingers gently stroked her.

He heard the faint catch in her breath.

"Drive faster, Serena."

A shiver worked over her body, then her gaze darted to the rearview mirror. "Are the cops behind—"

"No one's behind us." He wouldn't let fear control him. Or her. Adrenaline coursed through his body, and he knew it shook hers, too. They needed to channel that energy. Fight the fucking fear and focus on what would give them power to—

Screw it. This wasn't about power. It was about her. He wanted her. He wanted to fight the fear that whispered through his head and told him that he could lose her.

I won't lose her.

He'd take her. She'd take him. They'd go wild together.

His fingers inched up her leg. Paused near the juncture of her thighs. He swore he could feel the heat from her sex burning through the fabric.

"If...no one's following..." Her breath heaved in. "Then w-why? Why do I have to go faster?"

He pushed his fingers between her legs. Stroked the crotch of her jeans and loved the little moan that slipped from her lips. "Because it's time for us both to be satisfied." His fingers strummed against her, and a red flush brightened her cheeks.

The engine rumbled as her foot pressed down even harder on the accelerator.

"I love the way you drive," he murmured.

"And I love the way you touch me."

For a moment, his fingers stilled. Her honesty had just rocked straight to his core.

"Don't stop," Serena whispered, voice husky.

His fingers pressed to her again. The jeans were in the way. "When we get to your home, you're mine."

CHAPTER SEVEN

When her car screeched to a stop in front of her house, Serena wasn't thinking about dead bodies any longer. She wasn't thinking that a dead man's eyes could hold such shock, and she wasn't thinking that death felt cold. Far too cold. She'd thought of all that before. Back in that horrible storage room.

No, as she jumped from the car and she and Luis hurried up her steps, she wasn't thinking about death.

She thought of him.

Luis's touch. His body. The pleasure he'd soon give her.

The pleasure that would block the fear of the waiting cold. *The cold that wants to wrap around me and never let go.*

The front door slammed closed behind them.

Luis's hands settled on her hips. "How fast can you get naked?"

Ah, now that sounded like a challenge. She pulled away, cocked her head, and asked, "How fast can you?"

In a blink, he was naked. His clothes had vanished with just a wave of his hand.

Gotta love that magic.

Her gaze dropped to his chest. She loved his chest. So strong, with all those rippling muscles. His stomach was tight and flat. Luis's abs were a work of art.

His hand lifted, and his fingers grazed over his erection.

Oh, yes. The man was built. His cock — long and thick — bobbed toward her. Moisture gleamed on the broad head.

He was ready for her.

Her magic might be limited by the binding, but she still had a few tricks of her own. She waved her hands over her body, and her clothes and shoes disappeared.

Sometimes, it was good to be a witch.

When the devil wasn't after you.

She pushed the thought away as quickly as it rose. For just a few minutes, she wanted pleasure. Not fear. She needed the power she'd get from sex.

No, that was a lie. It wasn't just about power. It was...*I need him.* That truth was unsettling. Unnerving. She'd never wanted anyone so quickly. So completely. But then, she'd never met anyone quite like Luis.

His eyes heated as he looked at her. The gold gleamed so brightly. His cock swelled even more. They didn't have to worry about birth control, a nice little Other perk. Witches completely controlled their cycles, and as for soul hunters...

Immortals never caught illnesses of any sort.

He was the safest partner she'd ever had. And the most dangerous.

He reached for her.

Shaking her head, she caught his hand in hers. "I want a bed." She wanted cool sheets, a soft mattress, and him. She wanted Luis thrusting as hard and deep as he could between her thighs. Serena wanted him driving into her until the hungry ache in her sex had been assuaged.

"What my witch wants..."

She expected more magic. Wondered just what he was truly capable of doing. Could he move them by spell alone to her room or would he—

His arms wrapped around her and he pulled her up against his warm chest. His mouth swept down on hers. She loved the man's taste. Dark and rich and—

She was on the bed.

He sprawled over her, his mouth still locked to hers, and he pushed her against the mattress. His legs—the man had thick, muscled thighs that she'd love to ride—angled between hers so that Serena was spread wide for him. Her sex was open and already wet and so ready that she knew he had to catch the scent of her arousal. With his paranormal senses, how could he not?

He tore his mouth from hers. Luis turned his gaze toward her body. "Fucking gorgeous," he breathed. Then took her nipple with his mouth. Licked. Bit. Sucked.

Made her moan.

His fingers—she loved those clever fingers of his—parted the folds between her legs. His thumb pressed over her clit, and Serena nearly came off the bed.

"Easy…" A dark rumble.

But she didn't want it easy. Not with him. Hard, fast, bed-breakingly wild—that was how she wanted it.

And how she would take it.

Her nails dug into his back. Her thighs lifted and wrapped around his hips. "Hard." The demand snapped from her mouth.

His head jerked up. His mouth was wet. His lips parted.

She scored her nails down his back and pressed her hands into Luis's taut ass. "Wild."

His face hardened. "If that's what you want, then that's what I'll give you…"

The fingers that had caressed her sex stilled.

A wave of anticipation had her trembling.

Luis pulled back. The movement dislodged her legs from his hips. He brought his left hand up and curled his hand over her thigh. When his gaze dropped to her sex, she knew what he was going to do.

And she couldn't wait.

His shoulders pushed between her legs. His breath fanned over her exposed sex, and then he drove two fingers deep into her core. Every muscle in her body stiffened.

She opened her mouth to cry out, but the sound broke on her lips when Luis pressed his mouth against her. He locked his open lips over her clit. His tongue teased. Tasted.

Drove her wild.

His fingers thrust in and out, moving in a fast rhythm. First just the two, then a third large finger lodged inside of her.

He licked her. Swirled his tongue over the straining button of her desire. Then lapped up the moisture that pooled between her legs as the lust grew and grew. Serena felt the edge of his teeth. A light graze that had her freezing, then all but whimpering with pleasure when his tongue licked over her sex.

Her heart thudded in her ears and sweat slickened her body. The sunlight trickled through her blinds, and she watched Luis, unable to look away from the sight of his dark head between her thighs.

Her legs squeezed around him, clenching tight with every thrust of his hand. Her nipples stabbed into the air, her thighs trembled, and the promise of release beckoned, just seconds away.

"Luis." He was driving her crazy. And damn him, he was holding the control. Every single bit of control.

Time to break that control, time to —

His fingers withdrew — just when she was close — then he drove his tongue inside of her. The mounting tension erupted. Serena squeezed her eyes shut and threw her head back as the powerful spasms shook her.

Pleasure was power.

A secret every succubus and incubus knew.

And one that the witches used for their own gain.

Her eyes flashed open, and her lips parted on a sigh of satisfaction.

As the magic of the release filled her body, Luis moved. Rose above her. Pushed the head of his cock against her opening.

"Time to get wild, witch."

Wait, hadn't they already gotten — well, *she* had and —

He slammed into her. The force of his thrust was strong enough to send the bed sliding back against the wall. She was pretty sure she might have even heard the crack of breaking wood. *Wonderful.*

More than ready for him, Serena arched her hips and whispered his name.

His cock filled every inch of her and stretched muscles gone sensitive from her climax. He was big and even thicker than she'd thought, and he felt amazing. Once again, her legs clamped around his hips. As he began to move, rocking harder, driving deeper, she held on as fiercely as she could.

And Serena enjoyed the ride.

Their mouths met. Tongues thrust as hips jerked. Breaths panted. Their hearts raced. The spiral of lust built, built. His hands fondled her breasts. Teased her nipples and had her squirming beneath him.

When he rose, pulling that wonderful cock nearly out of her, her head lifted. Her fingers traced his nipples, then she licked him, loving the slightly salty taste of his skin.

They rolled, twisting and turning as they fought for release. For a pleasure that was just out of their grasp.

Serena settled on top of him. Her legs were on either side of his hips. Her sex clamped around his cock, and she could feel every inch of his arousal pulse inside of her.

His hands were on her hips. Holding too tightly, but she didn't care.

She squeezed him. Serena clamped down hard on his erection. Then, with a hiss of pleasure, she released her inner muscles.

His teeth ground together.

Another slow squeeze.

Now she had the control.

"Witch." Gritted. An accusation.

One she'd never deny.

Bending over him, she licked his nipples, drawing out the slow movements of her tongue, then glancing up at Luis from beneath her lashes.

His eyes glittered.

How do you like that, soul hunter? Do you —

In the next second, she was on her back again. Her legs splayed over his shoulders and he thrust fast, hard, and she was —

Exploding. A white-hot pulse of release ripped through her as Serena climaxed. Her whole body shuddered beneath him and the guttural cry that burst from her lips seemed to echo in the bedroom.

Lights danced before her eyes. Magic.

Pleasure.

Still, he thrust. Deeper.

The bed was a mess. Sweat coated their bodies.

Flesh to flesh. Sex to sex.

He swelled within her. Another hard inch, so thick now that the friction of his thrusts sent a stab of pleasure through her with each move of his body as aftershocks reverberated in her core.

"Serena." He drove even deeper. Froze. His gaze caught hers. For an instant, the molten gold of his eyes faded to pitch black.

Demon eyes.

The hot jet of his release filled her. The air in the room heated and brushed against her skin.

Pleasure is power. For the soul hunter, as well as the witch.

He shuddered against her. Her arms wrapped around him, and she clung to him. When the pleasure finally eased for them and their heartbeats began to slow, Serena stayed just where she was.

Right before she drifted to sleep, she could have sworn that their hearts were beating in perfect tune.

As if they were one.

***

Her aunt was in the middle of the circle of protection.

But the circle hadn't protected her.

Jayme Michaels lay on the ground, and her long, curling black hair cascaded around her face.

Serena ran to her. Fear tore through her.

No, no, not Aunt Jay. She was the strongest witch Serena had ever met. No one could harm her. Not human. Not Other.

Whoever was after Aunt Jay's coven, they couldn't have—

Her aunt's head was twisted. Her neck broken.

Her eyes were open. Her lips parted in surprise.

Serena skidded to a stop just outside of the sacred circle.

No, no, this wasn't right.

Not her aunt, not—

Serena awoke with a start. She jerked straight up in bed. Sunlight hit her hard in the face, and she turned away—

Only to have her gaze land on Luis's sleeping face. The sight of him wiped away the fog from her dream. No, not a dream. A nightmare.

She sucked in a deep breath. Her aunt hadn't looked like a broken doll when Serena had found her body. The fire had already gotten to her and destroyed her aunt's beauty by the time Serena had reached her.

Another deep breath.

The dream had come because of the body they'd found—she knew it. Pleasure had only been able to push aside the darkness for so long. Her hand reached for Luis. Hesitated.

His task was to stop the one after her. He would kill the warlock.

But she would not be useless in this battle...As she'd been in the fight to save Aunt Jay.

Her fingers curled into a fist.

Her powers wouldn't return full force until the binding was removed, and that blessed event wouldn't happen until the warlock drew his last breath. Death—either the bound victim's or the spell caster's—was the only way to remove a dark binding. Fortunately, she wasn't completely without magic, thanks in part to the furious pleasure she'd enjoyed with Luis.

She would not be helpless.

Luis would destroy the warlock.

But it would be up to her to find the bastard.

Serena eased from the bed. One of the wooden posts was broken, and the sight of it caused her to smile. Sex with Luis had been far unlike sex with any other partner. He'd consumed her.

Or, maybe they'd consumed each other. The pleasure had overwhelmed her. It would be far too easy to get addicted to that kind of pleasure.

As easy as it would be to become addicted to him.

No, she couldn't think that way. Serena grabbed a light silk robe and belted it across her waist. The day was slipping from them too quickly. Already, the clock on the bedside table told her it was long past noon.

Night would hold dangers. Perhaps another binding. The dark ones were always stronger at night.

Time for her to hunt now.

Carefully, she crept across the room. She made her steps as silent as possible because she didn't want to risk waking Luis. He wouldn't like what she planned to do with the vestiges of her magic, but that was just too bad.

Her power, her life.

The door closed behind her with a soft click.

***

Luis waited a moment. Listened to the faint footfalls as Serena disappeared down the hallway.

Then his eyes opened.

He drew in the scent of woman and sex. His cock was already erect. He'd gotten turned on just from the lingering traces of her sweet fragrance in the air.

What mischief was his dangerous little witch up to now?

He'd give her a few minutes, then he'd find out exactly what spells she was crafting so secretly. Serena should have realized that after their mating, there would be no more secrets.

The soul hunter had found the perfect soul that he wanted to take.

And she was just down the hallway.

CHAPTER EIGHT

Serena placed the items she and Luis had taken from the antique store in the middle of her living room. She'd pushed the furniture back moments before, the better to work.

Her fingers were steady as she positioned the candles around the witches' possessions. North. East. South. West. She lit the candles with a wave of her hand. She'd sat her scrying mirror down near the sofa. She picked it up, aware, as always, of the icy feel of the mirror in her hands.

Serena walked back toward the candles. Put the mirror at her feet. She drew in a deep breath, raised her hands high above her head and began her spell.

"Show me the one who used his spell,
To bind the witches I know too well.
Show me the man — show me the one
Whose magic I seek to have undone.
As I will,
So mote it be."

A simple spell. One that she wasn't certain would work. But the warlock had made a mistake. He'd worked magic on the items before her, and the dark magic he'd used left a faint taint. A touch of darkness.

A touch that would reflect him, if her spell worked.

The candles flickered around her.

Serena's gaze fell to the mirror. She watched as the surface darkened, as if black clouds were sweeping over the face of the mirror. Then the darkness moved faster and faster as the wind blew. Air brushed over her face. Sent the edges of her robe flapping back.

Her body trembled as she poured her magic into the spell and forced the image to sharpen. The strain made her whole body tremble. She wouldn't be able to last much longer.

Show me the one I seek.

The clouds thickened in the mirror. Pressed closer. Slowly began to form the face of a man.

Blue eyes stared up at her. Clear and sparkling. Dimples winked at her from the sides of his curving mouth. His blond hair blew, as if he, too, felt the breeze stirring in the closed room.

"Got you, bastard." Luis's voice rumbled from right behind her.

"Not yet," Serena muttered as she memorized that face. She'd make sure to never forget him. "But we will."

The candle flames died. Serena's arms dropped to her sides. Her gaze was still on the mirror and on the man who laughed up at her.

Luis's hands wrapped around her waist, and he pulled her tightly against him.

The grinning warlock slowly vanished.

Asshole, we're coming for you.

***

"He has more, you know." Luis picked up the tattered cloth that Serena had assured him several times was actually a swatch of Susan's quilt. "He wouldn't have left everything behind. If he had —"

"He wouldn't have been able to put the second bind on more of the coven, I know." Serena ran an agitated hand through her curling locks. He loved her hair. The wild curls. The soft, silky feel of the tresses under his fingers.

"Vanessa and Susan were both hit by the jerk this morning. So he has to have more of a stash." She hauled on her shoes. She'd dressed moments before, though he rather wished she'd just stayed in her silky blue robe. He liked the way it exposed the soft curves of her breasts.

Serena had been practically pulsing with rage since her spell. "The bastard's out there. You saw him, Luis. He's out there, and he's laughing at us."

Because he mistakenly thought he held the power. Fool. "We're just waiting for the night, Serena."

She slanted him a frown. "Why? Isn't that supposed to be his time?" Serena huffed out a breath. "Are we just going to be some kind of sitting ducks for this psycho?"

"No." He crossed his arms over his chest. Who did the lady think she was dealing with here? An amateur? "The night is my time, Serena. Mine more than any other being you'll ever meet." Vampires might have mistakenly thought they ruled. Demons could skulk in the shadows all they wanted, but he was the one who drew power with the setting of the sun.

Soon it would be time to use that power.

Her eyes sharpened with interest. "What's our plan?"

Our. Well, she had summoned him, and he'd given his word that she could hunt. But that had been before he'd learned what pain sounded like on her lips.

"We have two options, sweetheart."

Her foot tapped.

"As soon as night falls and the demons and vamps crawl out to stalk the city, we stalk them." It would be easy enough to catch the stench of the vampires—most of them smelled like decay. As for the demons, well, being part demon meant he could stare right through the veil of glamour that cloaked the majority of his kind. And he'd be able to smell them, too.

"And, uh, when we catch them?" She looked and sounded hesitant.

Probably because, unlike him, she didn't spend her nights stalking the psychotic demons most wanted to pretend didn't exist. But it never seemed to matter how many of the bastards he stopped. There were always more out there.

And Serena — she was proof of just how little good he could really do in this shit-screwed world. If she hadn't summoned him, he would have stayed in Mexico, finished his drink, then gone off to hunt the demon who'd been spotted in the area — the one who'd made a recent habit of hurting humans.

While he was hunting that demon, Serena would have died. *Serena would have died.*

There just weren't enough hunters in the world any longer. Too few to begin with. Too few left after the strongest, sickest paranormals had targeted his kind decades ago.

Maybe it was time for new blood.

His gaze caught Serena's.

"What do we do when we find the vamps?" Her nose scrunched in a way that made her look even cuter. "I hate the way those bloodsuckers are always staring at my neck."

He could understand that. Luis made a mental note to give serious pain to any vamps unlucky enough to be caught ogling Serena's gorgeous neck. He cleared his throat. "When we find them, we make them talk. A warlock strong enough to bind an entire coven — he'll be known by someone." Or something.

They just had to look in the right place. Or, in this case, the wrong one. The wrong side of town. The dangerous side. The side most humans inherently knew to stay away from when the sun set.

A deer could sometimes sense a hunter. Luis had learned in his lifetime that humans could all too often sense the Other that would prey on them. Not that the sensing usually did much good for them.

"Make them talk," she repeated slowly. Her head tilted, and her curls danced. "Are we going to have to hurt someone?" Her question didn't sound particularly concerned.

"Maybe a little," he allowed. *A lot.* But he'd be the one doing the hurting. Serena would keep her hands clean.

She nibbled on her lower lip. Fuck. Did the woman not understand just how badly he still wanted her?

Her tongue swiped out.

His cock jerked.

Business. Well, business should come first. But there were several more hours until dusk…

"What's our second option?" Serena asked.

The lust cleared a bit. He didn't like option two. Not a bit. "We wait for the third bind. Let the bastard think that he's broken your coven, and when he comes…" He shrugged and tried to look careless when he was starting to care too much, too quickly. *The way my father had fallen.* "I'll be waiting for him."

She backed up a step, and her shoulders hit the wall. "You—you mean you'd use me as bait."

Not the choice he wanted, but, if they couldn't track down the blond warlock, it might be their only option. "I wouldn't let him get to you, Serena." A promise.

"I'd be helpless!" She shook her head frantically. "One more bind on me, and I'm— I'm—"

"Human." Or as close as a woman like her would ever come to that fate.

"Yes! And we both know that if a bound witch dies while her powers are locked up inside of her—" She stopped, but he knew what she'd been about to say.

If a witch died while bound, the witch's killer took her powers at the moment of passing. "I wouldn't let him get to you," he repeated.

Serena didn't look convinced and her doubt pissed him off. Luis stalked toward her. She was already trapped against the wall. She'd trapped herself, so it wasn't like there was room for his witch to run. He crowded her deliberately, though, as he brushed his body close against hers. His arms rose, caged her, and his hands pressed against the white wall behind her head. "Do you trust me?"

She'd let him into that tempting body of hers just hours before. Let him take her with the hot passion that still burned him.

And made him ache for her.

She'd given him her body, yet when Luis asked his question, Serena hesitated. And *that* was his answer. A ball of anger unfurled in his gut. It was the answer he should have expected, but—

He wanted her trust. As much as he wanted her.

His head lowered over hers. "Do you trust me?" he repeated as he caught her scent, inhaling deeply.

"I-I don't know." *Truth.*

The anger within him flared brighter. "So you trust me enough to fuck, huh? But you don't trust me with your life—is that the way this game works?" Was it because of his mother? Because he'd failed before, did Serena not think that he could keep her safe? "I'm not gonna leave your side, witch—I won't leave you like I left her." He'd been on a hunt. Going after a djinn who'd slaughtered half a village. He hadn't realized his mother was in any danger. He'd thought she was safe and—

"Luis, no, I didn't mean—"

"Forget it." He shoved the memories of his past away and focused only on her. "Know this— I will keep you safe, whether you trust me or not.

I'll protect you and do my job of eliminating the warlock."

"Luis, I'm the one who summoned you, remember? That means —"

"Jackshit."

Her green eyes narrowed. Tension tightened her delicate body.

"You summoned me because you wanted a guard dog, and that's what you got, Serena. A fucking killer attack dog who would take anyone and everyone down before they had a chance to hurt you." He meant it. No one was going to sacrifice his witch.

No one.

Her lips parted and, hell, a man could only take so much temptation.

His mouth took hers. *Good enough to fuck.* Well, if that was the case, then he'd just go ahead and take his pleasure with her. She was wearing a skirt now. A short, black skirt that teased the tops of her thighs and made his cock pulse with arousal.

Luis drove his tongue into her mouth and pushed his left hand between her spread thighs.

Her gasp was swallowed by his mouth.

She twisted. Her body pushed against his. Her tight nipples stabbed into his chest. The witch wanted him. He'd caught the scent of her arousal even when she'd glared at him with sparks of anger in her gorgeous eyes.

When he touched the crotch of her soft cotton panties, his fingers felt her wet heat.

No preliminaries this time.

He was pissed with her for doubting him. With the blond asshole who was hunting her.

And he was hungry—for her. Her body. Her very soul.

It was his nature to hunt. To take. He wanted to take her more than he'd ever wanted anything in all of his centuries.

Serena's hands were on his shoulders. Not pushing away, but pulling him closer, and her mouth was wide and hungry on his.

The growl in his throat sounded just as he ripped her panties away.

"Luis!" Serena gasped out his name and gazed up at him with eyes gone dark with need.

Her folds were slick and swollen, primed with the same lust that hardened his cock. He pushed two fingers into her tight opening. He freaking loved the feel of her clenching sex around him.

She'd feel even better around his cock.

"Not here, Luis," she told him breathlessly. "We can—"

"Here." They were in the middle of her kitchen. Her blinds were up. Her windows wide open. He didn't really care. His fingers retreated, drove deep once more, and her head tipped back against the wall as she exhaled on a hard sigh.

Then she started to ride his hand.

A flush rose in the open vee of her shirt. Darkened her neck. Stained her glass-sharp cheeks.

Beautiful.

Her breath quickened as he watched her. Her hips jerked faster. Sexy witch. Sensual as a succubus.

His.

He drew his fingers away from her and had to bite back a fierce smile of pleasure when she shook her head in protest.

"I was so close!"

"Don't worry. I will fucking get you there." He wouldn't stop until she screamed with pleasure.

Her eyes were on him as he lifted his fingers to his lips and tasted her. A long, slow lick.

She swallowed.

"Later, I'm gonna have more of you." Later, she'd be spread beneath him again, and he'd lick her until he was drunk off her.

But for now…

His hand dropped to the front of his jeans. He popped open the button, eased down the zipper, and pulled out the cock that was twitching for the feel of her hot, tight sex.

"Put your hands on me," he ordered and his voice came out like a snarl. No help for that. He was living in a red haze of hunger. All for her.

Her hands slid down his body. Her touch was as soft as a butterfly. Slowly, she wrapped her fingers around his dick. Serena squeezed him, then pumped his straining length with a long stroke, from root to head.

Again.

Again.

It took all of his control not to come in her hands. He grabbed her hips. Luis was aware that his hold was too tight, too rough, but he couldn't ease his grip.

No damn way.

Luis lifted her and pinned her back even harder against the wall. Her legs were up, her sex open, and her hands still pumped him.

Fuck.

"Guide me in," he ordered, voice a rumble. "Take me deep inside, Serena. Let me watch you…"

Her skirt was bunched at her waist. Her sex was flushed pink and glistening.

He wanted another taste.

Her fingers tightened around him.

His hips thrust forward helplessly as sweat slid down his back.

Serena guided the head of his cock toward her body. Straight toward the tight opening that quivered for him. When he felt the first brush of her creamy, hot core along his cock, Luis clenched his back teeth.

Control won't be lasting much longer.

Every instinct he possessed screamed for him to thrust forward, as hard and deep as he could go. But he wanted to watch her. Wanted to watch as he slid slowly into her body.

"Luis…" His name whispered on a breath.

The sound of his name coming from her lips. The need in her voice…

Ah, hell —

He slammed balls deep into her.

And immediately felt Serena's sex begin to spasm around him as she came. His spine prickled. Her contractions were silky, strong, and squeezed him even better than her hand. He pulled back, then drove deep.

Retreated.

He plunged deep.

Luis heard her strangled cry of pleasure.

Felt the bite of her nails on his skin.

He wanted her to come again. With him. Her legs locked around his hips and he pumped into her, driving as fiercely as he could for the rush of release that he knew was waiting.

The ripples of her sex continued. She moaned and shuddered against him. "Luis. Luis. Luis!"

He felt the second climax hit her because the pleasure hit him, too. Semen jetted from him, and spilled deep into her body as he came. He drove into her and held tightly to Serena. The power of his release had his knees trembling, his breath rasping out, and the room shaking around them as his magic and power surged through the kitchen.

The release went on, and the pleasure filled every cell in his body. *Pleasure is power.* Power for his witch. Power for him.

His gaze met hers as the aftershocks began to ease. Her lips were blood red. A tear tracked down her cheek. For a moment, his heart seemed to stop. Had he hurt her?

Then her mouth curved and her hand released its fierce grip on his shoulder to slide down his chest. Her fingers paused right over the heart that raced for her.

"Again," Serena sensually ordered.

And the already swelling cock inside of her was happy to oblige. After all, only a fool would deny a witch's demand.

She yanked off his shirt. Her mouth locked on his nipple, and he thrust deep into her wet heat.

Luis had never thought of himself as a fool.

CHAPTER NINE

Night found them on the streets. Walking in the darkness on the side of town that most didn't even realize existed.

Buildings stood as battered shells. Boards lined the windows of the closed shops. A few burning garbage cans spit flames into the sky and chased a bit of the darkness away.

In the distance, a drum pounded with a furious, driving beat.

There were supernatural clubs in the city. Places that the Other frequented. They were close—close enough for Luis to smell the blood in the air. The blood that would lure the vampires.

They weren't heading to those clubs. No, their prey wouldn't be inside. The monsters they sought were on the streets. Waiting. Planning. Hunting. Just as Luis was.

"Hate to be a mood killer, but didn't we have this whole talk already about using me as bait?" Serena groused as she slanted him a simmering glance. "And I distinctly remember not being on team go-for-it." She stood just under one of the few street lights that actually worked. Her arms were crossed over her chest. One booted foot tapped on the broken sidewalk.

He waited a few feet behind her. He'd pressed his body close to the cold brick wall so that he could be completely hidden by the shadows.

"We did have that talk," he conceded. "And we both agreed you weren't going to be bait for the warlock." She wouldn't be. Not unless that dark choice became absolutely necessary.

And in that case, he would protect her. He wouldn't fail again.

"Yeah, that's what I thought. So why the hell am I the one standing out here all defenseless with come-and-get-me written on my forehead?"

Simple. Because the woman looked like perfect prey in the dark sweater that cupped her full breasts and in the jeans that clung all too well to her great ass and legs.

"It's easier to get the Other to come to us this way." Or, rather, to her. The ones he was hunting, they'd love to get their hands on a tasty treat like her. Deceptively innocent, with her wide eyes and nervous hands, she'd bring the bastards right to her.

"Aren't they going to sense you?" she pushed as she nervously tucked a lock of hair behind her ear. "Demons can sense each other, you said it yourself—"

"No one will sense me." Not even a level-ten demon would be able to pick up his power trail.

"Don't forget, I'm not a full-blooded demon." At his words, Luis thought he saw her shiver.

She rocked forward. "So everything I've ever heard about you—it's true, isn't it? Your kind—soul hunters—you're born when a witch and level-ten demon mate. You're immortal."

"Yes." Immortality was a blessing and a curse. Everyone else died. He didn't. He wouldn't. It was so hard to watch the people he loved slip away.

But it was easy to watch the assholes he stalked pass from this realm. They deserved death. But when it was the good ones, like his mother—

"How many of your kind are there, Luis?" Her voice drifted to him.

Too few. "Less than there were a hundred years ago." Luis realized he hadn't seen another of his kind in what—five, ten years?

He'd been too busy killing to count.

And too busy fighting to stay alive.

Just because a being had been graced with the ability to live forever, well, that didn't mean some smart bastard couldn't come along and figure out the secret to his death. Everyone and everything could die, but the real trick in this world was figuring out just how to kill the monsters.

"Is it true that you can't be hurt by mortal weapons?"

He coughed. "That rule is for level-ten demons." And, since he was part demon, yes, weapons forged by man couldn't hurt him.

"So, what? You have to have your heart cut out? Get beheaded?" Her small foot was back to tapping against the broken sidewalk.

She'd just listed all the old immortal-killing standbys. Luis sighed. "It's complicated." Mostly because he was complicated. "And I'm not going to explain it now. Wrong part of town for this talk." Definitely the wrong time, too.

But his witch was on the right track. If his head was severed and if his heart was cut from his chest—while it still beat—and if his head and heart were burned to ashes, then, yes, he'd finally die. That was the magic combo. A very hard combo for his enemies to achieve.

"Has anyone ever almost...killed you?" Serena's hesitant question was softer than the others had been. Her gaze wasn't on him. It was on the shadows on the opposite end of the street.

No monsters were there.

He'd sensed no threats on the street yet, so he'd let Serena keep up her questions because he knew that she was afraid. And he'd discovered that when she was nervous or afraid, his witch liked to talk. A rather cute trait, and one that he'd allow for a few more moments.

Just until the demons came out.

"Yes, sweetheart, I've almost been killed a few times." Those panther shifters in South

America had actually come pretty close to taking him out of this world. One had swiped at his chest with razor sharp claws while another had gone for his neck, slicing right at Luis's jugular.

He'd bled too much, gotten too weak, but still managed to rip through the pack. Then he'd healed, as was his nature. And lived to fight and kill another day.

Or night.

Like tonight.

"Have you ever been afraid?" Her voice was even softer now, and, still, she didn't glance his way. He was angled diagonally behind her, so he could just make out the faintest movement of her lips.

"Once or twice." With her.

And on that long-ago day when he'd rushed to save his mother, only to arrive far too late.

Her head jerked toward him, "Luis, I—"

"Quiet." Power was in the air, flickering. They weren't alone any longer.

His eyes narrowed as he watched Serena take in a deep breath. Her attention turned back to the dark street.

She wouldn't see the one coming for her…

But Luis already had the demon in his sights.

CHAPTER TEN

This will not end well. Serena hunched in front of the light post, because, yes, standing underneath that freaking beacon was such a fine plan.

Every psycho in the area would be after her. Just what Luis wanted.

The warmth had seeped from the city with the fall of night. The temperatures had taken a serious nosedive from the warmer weather of previous days, and Serena shifted her stance a bit as she rubbed her hands together in an attempt to ward off the growing chill in the air.

A week ago, she wouldn't have been afraid. She would have used her power to blast any idiot stupid enough to confront her all the way across the street and into that busted building that looked like an old pawnshop.

A week ago.

Now, she had to rely on Luis, and relying on someone else wasn't exactly her strong suit. *But that's why I summoned him — because I knew he could help me.* She just hadn't realized he'd be doing the whole "bait" routine with her.

Immortal jerk.

And just where was the paranormal he'd sensed? She couldn't see anyone. Didn't hear anything but the crackle of flames — and who had lit those fires anyway? No one was around but —

"Lost, witch?"

The voice came from her left. Whispered into her ear.

Blood of the goddess.

Serena swallowed. Straightened her shoulders. *The boogeyman's got my back.* He'd better. "I'm not the least bit lost," she answered slowly. Serena was proud that her voice didn't shake even a little. She turned her head toward the predator who'd snuck so close, and she lifted one brow. "Are you?"

One glance was more than enough to tell her that this guy — yes, he was most definitely lost. His eyes were coal black. Every single bit of his eyes — a demon stare. Usually, demons cloaked their eyes with a glamour and made the color appear like a human's. The true black color only appeared when their emotions and passions were high — like when Luis's gaze had flashed black on her during their wild mating.

But this fellow — he wasn't bothering with glamour. No, he was letting his gleaming black eyes show to the world.

His face was long and angular. Too pale. Bloodless. His teeth were sharp, and they shouldn't have been. What the hell? His teeth were all narrowed to points, like a vamp's fangs.

Serena realized the demon before her had deliberately filed his teeth. The better to kill?

She balled the hands that wanted to shake into tight fists. *Where's my power when I need it?*

The answer, of course, was tied up in a warlock's web.

"Seems I've just found the thing I was looking for tonight." He smiled at her and flashed those wicked teeth. Then his gaze raked over her body.

Hell. Just what she didn't need. Bloodlust and physical lust. A dangerous combination.

"I would have preferred a human. They scream so very loudly, you know."

She wanted to scream right then. Scream for the demon to get the hell away from her. No, not just away. Out. Out of the city. Out of the whole country.

Her skin crawled as she stared at him. He wore a long black coat and dark pants. His hair was slicked straight back from his forehead, and his fingers—they were bony, with long and thick nails. Nails that, even in the weak light, she could see were stained red.

"You-you're not from around here, are you?" Serena hated that the faintest tremble had entered her voice. Okay, so every time the jerk opened his mouth, she smelled death. No need to freak out about that fact.

After all, her bodyguard was just a few feet away.

And Luis had been right — the demon didn't sense him, at all.

Perhaps the creep was too focused on her to even see the danger that waited.

The demon laughed. "No, this is my first...trip...to your city." He lifted a hand toward her, and Serena steeled herself. "I think I'm going to have so much fun here."

Don't be so sure of that. At the last second, Serena stepped back so that she missed the touch of his gnarled fingers. "What makes you think I'm a witch?" she asked as her mind jumped back to the first words he'd spoken to her. Demons didn't normally have the ability to recognize her kind and —

"Because you're bound," he replied, and his nostrils flared. "I can smell the marks on you. Every demon and shifter in the city can." Another chilling smile. "Poor witch. No magic, and all alone."

"Not exactly," she snapped back and lifted her chin. If that jerk tried to touch her again —

"Oh, exactly. You're exactly what I want." Not a smile any more. His face had gone feral. "Let's hear you scream —" His claws came at her.

Serena jumped away.

Luis bounded from the shadows. "Let's here you scream, demon." He grabbed the demon and spun the bastard around.

"What the—aw, fuck!"

"Hello, Jack."

Jack? Serena stumbled back a few more feet. If Luis knew the guy *by name*, the demon had to be trouble. The kind she didn't want.

"What are you doin' here?" the demon grated. "Last I heard, you were hunting in Mexico—"

"And that's why you thought it was safe to come out of hiding, huh?" Luis moved in one of his too-fast-to-see whirls. When Serena blinked, she found him holding the demon up against the light post. Luis's fingers were locked around the creep's throat. "Mistake, Jack. Big mistake. It's never safe for you to be on the streets. Not safe for the humans, the paranormals, and damn sure not safe for you."

The demon's eyes began to bulge.

"Uh, Luis…" Serena shuffled a little closer to him.

He didn't glance her way. Not that she blamed him. Luis was dangling a bastard demon two feet up in the air and slowly choking the life from him. He was obviously kinda busy, but they *had* come out on these streets for a reason.

"You're weak, Jack. Only a level-four." Luis made a clicking sound with his tongue. "Is that why you go after the humans? Because you feel powerful with them?"

Jack tried to gasp out a reply, but the wheezing wasn't much of a response.

When his face started to purple, Serena continued her forward shuffle movements. "Luis, we're not here for this. The warlock —"

Jack's bulging black eyes slanted toward her.

"Don't fucking look at her!" Luis's roar shook the street.

The demon's eyes flew back to Luis.

Serena reached out and touched Luis's back. Felt the rock-hard, battle-ready tension in him. "The warlock," she repeated. She didn't know what Luis's past was with this Jack jerk, and, yes, the demon creeped the hell out of her, but they had to find out about the bastard after her.

A shudder passed over Luis's body. "You answer my questions," he snarled at the demon, "and you tell me the truth." He rammed Jack's head back into the light pole. Metal groaned. "Got it?"

The demon's lips formed "Yes," but no sound escaped him.

"Stay behind me, Serena," Luis ordered.

Fine with her. She wasn't interested in getting any closer to the demon. He knew that she was bound. Well, partially bound. Easy prey.

Slowly, Luis lowered the demon. Jack's feet touched down with a soft sigh. Luis eased his hold, but didn't completely move his fingers away from the demon's throat. "I'm looking for a warlock."

"L-lot of 'em h-here..." Jack said, voice hoarse.

"Blond. Blue-eyed. One that makes a habit of hanging out with charmers."

Jack blinked. "D-don't k-know h-him. J-just got in-into t-town…"

Luis laughed and the sound chilled Serena. She was glad that she couldn't see his face. But over Luis's shoulder, she could see the demon's face — and the fear that flashed over it.

Luis lifted his hand, and Serena saw claws spring from his fingertips. What the hell? Shock froze her. How did Luis have claws? He wasn't a shifter.

Before Serena could say a word, Luis slashed the demon's face. Left side. Right. Long, jagged marks dripped blood as the demon howled in pain.

"Wrong answer," Luis murmured.

Jack whimpered.

"Now, let's try again, Jack, and, remember, I can tell when you lie to me."

He could tell when the demon lied — oh, crap! If that was true, then it meant Luis was a detector. She'd heard of them before. Beings who could hear truth and lies, but she'd never actually met someone like that before. *Well, um, I guess I have now.* Met one. Had wild sex with one.

"Lie to me one more time," Luis's voice was a dangerous rumble, "and I will carve open your throat."

The demon started talking, fast. "H-he's in one of th-those big, white houses, w-with columns, f-fancy, in R-Roswell—"

The name clicked instantly in Serena's mind. Roswell. The antebellum homes. Historic district.

"G-got a b-big, bl-black gate, iron. N-name's Michael...something. D-didn't know y-you...were af-after him—"

"But you knew he liked to hunt witches."

"Y-yes..."

Luis shook his head. "You knew, but you didn't care, did you, Jack? Because you had hunting of your own to do."

Jack didn't reply to that statement.

Serena figured that was probably answer enough.

"Do you hunt witches?" Luis pushed. "Do you kill them? Do you kill the weak? Do you—"

"Every fucking chance I get!" The answer seemed torn from Jack.

Serena gaped in shock as his eyes doubled in size and he gasped out, "Fuck me, fuck me! I-I can change! I can stop, I can—"

"Turn away, Serena," Luis directed, and his voice was ice cold.

Jack's lips trembled. "N-no, witch, d-don't, he'll—"

"Turn away, Serena."

Her shoulders stiffened. "I'm not your pet bitch, Luis. Remember that when you talk to me."

He finally shifted to stare at her as he fired a glance over his shoulder. His eyes were as black as Jack's. "Please, Serena." His voice was softer. For her? "Don't watch me do this."

She spun on her heel.

The fast and desperate cries of the demon rang in her ears.

Almost helplessly, Serena peered back —

Luis had freed the demon's neck. Jack was shrinking back against the post. Luis lifted his hands, palms up. The flesh of his hands — it glowed and —

She jerked her gaze away when his fingers landed on the demon's shoulders.

The scream that she heard had her choking back her own cry.

Don't look. The order was her own this time.

But she looked anyway. A witch's curiosity was a dangerous thing. A weakness most of her kind shared. So her head turned and her eyes flickered back and she saw the darkness of Jack's eyes fade to a stark white. Heard the last rasp of his breath leave his body. Then Serena watched as Luis lifted his hands. The dead demon dropped to the ground with a thud.

"I told you not to watch." Emotionless.

Her gaze snapped to him. "Luis..."

His eyes were still black and a faint glow seemed to light his flesh from the inside out.

"Witches...always curious, just like the damn cats you all used to be so sickeningly fond of." He spared a glance for the demon on the ground. "I hope you're burning somewhere now, bastard."

Then he turned his back on the demon and fully faced her.

Her heart hammered in her chest, and Serena realized her palms were slick with sweat. Not cold any longer, she was burning hot. Fear could do that to a woman.

Luis lifted his right hand, and Serena jerked back. *He'd just killed a demon with only a touch.*

Luis's mouth tightened. "You knew what I was when you summoned me, Serena."

Yes, yes, she'd known. But knowing and *seeing* him in action were two different things.

"You knew then, and you knew when you fucked me."

It was hard not to flinch at his words.

His hand was still in the air between them. Regular nails now, thank the goddess, but..."I don't understand." She cleared her throat because her voice sounded too weak — and she didn't want to be weak. "How did your hands change? Soul hunters aren't shifters and — "

His fingers balled into a fist. "I've killed shifters. Dozens of them. Demons. Djinn. The ones who stalked the world, determined to torture and murder, I stopped them." Slowly, he uncurled his fist and his fingers, as they extended, had what looked to be about four-inch long claws sprouting from their tips. "Most don't understand. They think all I do is kill, but I'm a soul hunter. I hunt, and I take the powers that lurk in the souls of the Other, so that when they leave this world, they go out as helplessly as humans."

I take the powers that lurk in the souls. Oh, shit. Shit. A cold knot formed in her gut. "You mean — all the beings you kill — "

"I get their power." A shrug. His claws vanished in a blink. "Think of my touch as a binding spell. Instead of the three marks, it just takes the grasp of my hand, and any Other becomes helpless. When the powers drain away, the body dies." His lips twisted. "And my job is done."

No regret. No guilt. "You just…kill." No, he drained powers first, then he killed. Her gaze darted to the fallen demon. She shuddered.

He killed.

Just like the warlock who was after her.

Her arms wrapped around her stomach. "Why did you kill him?" Okay, yes, the demon had scared the hell out of her, but other than making her heart jump into her throat, he hadn't actually done anything to her and —

"Jack fancied himself a modern-day copy of the original."

Serena shook her head and forced her gaze back to him. *Stop looking at the dead demon.* "I don't know what you're — "

"Jack the Ripper."

She blinked.

"He liked to slash his victims apart just like the original Ripper, except he didn't go after prostitutes. He went after humans or weak paranormals. Then he had a good old time making them scream as he sliced up their bodies."

Let's hear you scream. Serena rocked back. "You knew who he was the moment you first sensed him, didn't you?" He'd known, and he'd let her stand there and talk to a freaking sadistic killer.

One who wanted to make her scream.

A grim nod. "You were never in any danger. I would not have—"

"Asshole!" Maybe it was a good thing she didn't have her full magic right then—she would have tried to fry the jerk. "How many times do I have to tell you, I'm not bait?" Her hands were at her sides now, fisted, because she really, really wanted to slug him.

All powerful soul hunter or not.

"Serena—" Luis stepped forward and reached for her.

She threw out a spell. Sent the air swirling around her as a force field sealed her away from his touch.

His fingers slammed into the invisible wall. His eyes turned to furious slits. "Serena."

Her brow furrowed as she fought to hold the field. It was weak as hell, but she was making a point! "Don't use me, Luis!"

His fist punched against the field. "I'm trying to save your life!"

"You could have warned me about Jack, you could have—"

"I didn't know that SOB would be hunting here. By the time I realized it was him, it was too late, and he hunts by sensing fear. If I'd told you what was happening and how easily I could take him down, your emotions would have changed and he would have sensed it."

Her temples began to throb. The force field she'd created was getting even weaker. "I don't want to be bait," she repeated, but this time, she was talking about the warlock. Or maybe she'd been talking about him all along. Her hand rubbed her right temple. "I don't want to be bound."

"I am with you, Serena. No one is going to hurt you. No one."

"I want to protect myself." She always had. "I don't want to be weak." As weak as the pitiful spell that wasn't really holding him off. Serena knew Luis could have broken through her force field with one push of magic.

But he hadn't.

"You're not going to be weak," he promised, and his hand flattened on the field. "We're going to get the bastard, you're going to be safe, and I swear, I'll return you to full power."

Her hand lifted and hovered over his. "Why did you agree to help me?" She'd summoned him, but he could have left at any time. He could have laughed in her face and vanished.

A muscle flexed along his hard jaw. "Because I wanted you." Power filled his words. "From the first glimpse through the fog, I wanted you."

And she'd wanted him.

"Trust me, Serena. Trust me to save you. Trust me to—" He broke off, shaking his head.

For a moment, her gaze again dropped to the body of the dead demon. Goose bumps rose on her arms.

Luis had spent lifetimes battling demons like Jack. Fighting to keep the world safe. Fighting alone. Always alone. "Why do you do it?" she whispered. "The council is long gone. It's not your duty to keep fighting these bastards." Though she'd screamed that it was his job the first time they'd met. But it wasn't. He was entitled to live a life just like everyone else. So why did he do it? Why keep fighting the darkness?

"Because someone has to," he replied simply. "And I'm one of the only beings strong enough to face those in the dark."

Her heart pounded so hard that her chest hurt. Was it truly that simple for him? And, goddess, but what must his life be like? So many battles. So much evil.

"Serena…" A plea was in his voice now, with even a touch of…desperation? "Trust me."

She forced her gaze away from the demon. Met Luis's stare. Her lover with the golden eyes and the touch of death. The man who fought evil, when others would have run. Trust him? Oh, yes, she did. With her life.

And with her soul.

As her spell faded with a whisper of air, her fingers curled over his. "I do trust you."

CHAPTER ELEVEN

He got her off that street and away from the body as fast as he could. Luis didn't worry about disposing of the demon. The demons who frequented the area would make Jack vanish.

Another bastard off his list. A particularly nasty and sadistic killer.

When he'd caught the demon's scent and realized who was out stalking, he'd nearly lost it. Almost let his power rip out full force. He hadn't wanted Serena close to that sonofabitch. Hadn't wanted Jack to so much as look at her.

But he'd known that if any Other in the city knew about the warlock, it would have been a piece of shit like Jack. So he'd held on to his control as long as he could. He'd let Serena lure the guy in, and when Jack had made the mistake of reaching for Serena, Luis had attacked.

He hadn't wanted Serena to see him make the kill.

When she looked at him, sometimes, he'd catch a hint of fear or worry in her eyes.

But she often just looked at him as if he were...a man. He wanted her to keep looking at him that way. Wanted her to always look at him as if he were just her lover.

And not the killer she'd summoned.

His body was bursting with energy. The power of the death touch ran through him. Pulsed in his veins. The demon's energy blended with his own and sent currents of magic pumping through him. The magic was powerful. Heady. Almost uncontrollable. It seemed to boil through his body. The rush was greater than any adrenaline surge could ever be. Usually after a kill with his death touch, he found a woman. Got between her legs and rode hard and fast for the rest of the night until the power burned away.

He felt the same wild need now, the same lust.

But he didn't just want any woman.

He wanted the woman who sat so stiffly beside him as she drove her car, streaking down the streets and racing through the darkness. The woman who had touched him after a kill and said she trusted him.

Truth.

"Luis..." Serena's voice was husky.

He glanced over at her.

"Something's...wrong."

He tried to unclench his fingers from their white-knuckled grip on the door handle.

"Are you all right?" she asked.

She hadn't lied to him. He wasn't about to lie to her. "I will be." Once the edge of tension wore off.

In about eight or nine hours.

Fuck.

She braked at a red light. Turned to face him. "Tell me what's happening. You're stiff as a board over there. You're sweating, and you haven't moved in fifteen minutes. Are you sick? Are you—"

"It's after…effects." The only weakness his kind had. The energy from the kill pumped through his body too hard. Too fast. The result was a furious tension and a ravenous sexual hunger.

Now that he thought about it, his hunger for Serena was always pretty ravenous.

The light changed to green, but Serena didn't take her foot off the brake. "What does that mean?" she pushed. "Do you need to rest? To eat or to—"

"Fuck."

She blinked. "Oh. That, um, wasn't exactly next on my list of guesses."

No lies. Not between them. Not to her. "To get back to being one hundred percent, I need to fuck. I need to get you naked, and take you over and over until the power shock fades, and I'm close to normal." Normal for him was a relative thing. Grimly, he added, "And maybe then I can stop breathing without my cock twitching for you."

Her lips parted. "Ah…I…see."

Probably not. She didn't understand that he was literally drowning in her scent, that talking was hard, and that with every breath he took, he tasted her.

And that he wanted to fuck her so badly he ached.

She glanced around the darkened streets. Gave a nod, then punched the gas and spun the steering wheel to the left.

"Serena!"

Tires squealed.

She didn't glance his way. "You want me."

Hell, yes.

"You need to have sex to…work through this tension."

He needed to have sex because he wanted inside her. But, yeah, getting past the power surge was necessary, too.

"My art studio is a few blocks away. I had to get a place to meet with my clients. It's not real big, but if you don't mind the paint and the lack of a bed—"

If he could have her, he wouldn't mind a damn thing.

"Then we can be there in two minutes." She glanced at him, and Luis was caught by the desire he saw in her emerald stare. One that was almost a match for his own ferocious need. "And you can have me in three."

Hell, yes.

CHAPTER TWELVE

The scent of paint hit him the moment Serena unlocked the door to the small loft.

"I rented here because the light is so good. My clients like the studio, and I like to have a separate place for doing their work." She flipped on the lights.

Luis tried to bite down on his hunger for her and focus on his surroundings. Her art was on the walls. Intense power. Proud passion. "You're damn good, Serena."

Her lips parted in surprise.

He wanted to kiss her. To taste her. *To take and take and never let go.*

"Ah, thanks. Painting—it's almost like magic to me." She smiled at him, a sweet, real smile.

His heart lurched.

Ah, hell...No way was he going to be able to wait much longer. Or, wait at all. Luis dragged her into his arms. Kicked the door closed and took her mouth. He kissed her with a fury and a ravenous need. He started stripping off her clothes. Heard the thud of her boots as she kicked them to the floor.

He wasn't going to take the time to strip. He unbuckled his pants, shoved them out of the way, caught his straining cock and —

"Let me," Serena breathed the words against his mouth.

Then she pulled back and dropped to her knees before him.

"Serena." A few drops of liquid pulsed from the tip of his dick.

Her fingers closed around him. Squeezed. Stroked. She seemed to know exactly how to touch him and make the dark lust grow even more. His knees trembled as his cock jerked eagerly in her grasp.

Her lips curved. Parted.

Then she bent her head toward him — her luscious red mouth opened — and took him inside.

His teeth clenched as a ragged groan burst from his lips.

She moved her head and sucked. Her cheeks hollowed as she drew on him. She tasted and savored and drove him fucking insane.

Stars danced before his eyes. His fingers sank into the riotous mass of her curls. So damn soft. And her mouth was so hot. "Baby, you need to stop. I'm going to — "

She let him go. "I want you. I want to taste all of you."

His control shredded as she drew him in deep, then pulled back to lick the head of his arousal. Serena swirled her tongue over his cock. Gave another long, deep suck.

Then she swallowed.

Fuck, fuck, fuck. There was no holding back. There was only savage need. Consuming lust. He started moving her, faster, harder, thrusting his cock past her silken lips.

She swallowed again.

Luis came in her mouth. He roared her name and shuddered helplessly as she drank in his release.

When she'd wrung every drop from his body, she pulled away. Leaned back and watched him.

Luis stared down at her.

His cock began to swell again. *I will always want her. Again and again. Endlessly.*

What looked like white sheets were draped across the floor behind her. Paint spotted the material. Luis figured the sheets would be better than the floor.

"Take off the rest of your clothes, witch." She'd bewitched him with nothing more than a touch the first night they'd met. Enslaved him with a smile. He knew the truth now. He would never, ever get enough of her.

Serena laughed as she pushed off her panties and then stretched her body on the cloth. "Someone is ready for more fun." Her eyes danced with hunger and sensual power.

Power...because she'd just broken a soul hunter's control.

He dropped to his knees before her. Kissed the delicate inside of her ankle. One, then the other. Licked his way up the silky-smooth skin of her leg. "I will always be ready for more of you." He wanted to hear Serena scream his name.

And what a soul hunter wanted…

He got.

Luis parted her legs. Stroked his fingers over her clit. When he touched her, when he caressed her so carefully, Serena's back arched off the floor.

A good start. But he could do better than that. She'd just given him mind-blowing pleasure. She deserved the same. No, more. She deserved everything.

He put his mouth on her and fucking worshipped her with his lips and tongue.

Her moan was so sweet.

But he wanted more. His tongue stroked over her. Licked. Fast, hard licks. Then short, slow swipes.

She began to call his name.

But not to scream for him. Not yet.

He pushed two fingers inside her. Felt the delicate muscles of her sex clamp greedily around him. He withdrew his fingers, then drove them into her again, going knuckle deep, before retreating.

Her hips jerked faster as she pushed closer and closer to him.

Luis still wanted more.

He pulled his fingers free. Lowered his mouth. Touched her trembling flesh with the tip of his tongue.

Then drove his tongue inside of her.

The scream she gave as Serena came for him was music to his ears.

***

Luis thrust his cock into her just as the last tremors of her climax faded.

Serena stared up at him. Lines of tension and need were etched onto his face. A dark power drove him. She could feel the magic in the air. But there was more. The hunger she felt for him, the stark lust she'd experienced nearly from the beginning, was reflected in his eyes.

Power to power.

Lover to lover.

Sex to sex.

She locked her legs around him. Held on tight as he slammed into her and drove that thick cock of his deep into her. Her sex clamped around him. Clutched tight and a flash of pleasure had her undulating beneath him.

Then he thrust harder. Curled his hands around her hips and lifted her into his strokes.

His eyes began to darken as he gazed down at her.

The pleasure built again.

She didn't look away from him. Couldn't. Serena tightened around him and rode his cock as wildly as she could. When the next climax hit her, she didn't even try to muffle her cry of release.

But then, neither did he.

***

She slept at some point. After she rode him long and hard with her breasts bouncing as she took his cock inside. After he flipped her onto her stomach and took her with her hands digging into the paint-stained sheets.

She slept, and he watched her. His fingers traced the star on her belly. Such a beautiful, simple design. One witches had long used. *I don't want to be weak.* Her words played through his mind.

His little witch didn't understand. Even without her magic, she wouldn't be powerless. She was smart, resourceful, and brave. Not many would have stood beneath that streetlight and waited for a demon to walk from the darkness.

And not many would have risked using dark magic to summon a soul hunter.

He brushed his face against her curls. Inhaled her scent.

I don't want to be weak. His head lifted. His mother had been weak, at the end. Life was too short for so many.

He put his hand back over Serena's stomach. Power and a dark need still filled him. But his control was back, and it would hold, no matter how much his witch tempted him. He had a promise to keep and a warlock to kill.

She shifted against him, and her eyes blinked open. "Luis?"

Bending, he pressed a kiss to her sleep-softened lips. "We have to go, sweetheart." There were only about two more hours of darkness left.

Just enough time to finish this battle.

Understanding filled her eyes as the mist of dreams faded. "We're going after him."

"You won't worry another night about the warlock." He pulled away from her, found his clothes scattered on the floor, and began to dress.

Serena sat up slowly. "And then you'll go away. Back to—wherever the hell you were before, huh?" A touch of anger had entered her voice.

Yes, he'd go back to Mexico. He had another rogue demon with a death wish to track.

There was always someone to track.

He picked up Serena's clothes. Handed them to her. "Our deal will be over."

Her eyes narrowed. "You'll just walk away." The words were bitten out from between her teeth.

Luis frowned. "What do you want from me, Serena?" What did she want that he had not given? He'd fight with his last breath for her. He would kill for her.

"I want more than you can give." She swiped at her eyes.

Oh, hell, was Serena crying?

"This wasn't supposed to happen!" She jumped up and jerked on her clothes. She didn't look at him. "You were supposed to come here, help me, leave and not—" Her words tumbled to a halt as Serena shook her head. "Forget it. Let's go get the warlock and end this."

End this. Her words echoed in his mind.

Not yet. "What wasn't I supposed to do, Serena?" The question was important. He didn't want to have failed her. Not when she'd given him a glimpse of life. Passion. Warmth.

Things he hadn't felt or seen in centuries.

Her chin notched up. "Care. Okay, asshole? Happy now? You weren't supposed to make me care."

He stilled. Serena was telling the truth. She did care for him, but there was more. The way her words vibrated with—

"This is stupid!" Another hard swipe with her hand over her cheek. "Look, just forget it. I'm scared. I'm tired. I'm trapped in some weird lust-land with you and I don't know what the hell I'm saying." She tugged on her boots. Hopped a bit. "Just forget—"

His hands caught her and held her steady. "I'm not ever going to forget you."

For a moment, her lips trembled. Then she pressed them together and shook her head.

He freed her and stepped back.

"You will," she replied with her voice steady and her eyes wide. "When years pass and I'm nothing more than ashes, and you're still living, you'll forget me. Just like you've probably forgotten so many others and—"

"I've never forgotten." The snarl burst from him and the room trembled with his power. "Not a soul I've taken. Not a loved one I've lost."

Her breath hitched. "Luis..."

"You're wrong if you think immortality is easy. It's not. It's not fun, and it's sure as hell not pretty. It's dark and it's cold. It's finding villages torn to the ground by fucking killers—and seeing the bodies of innocents left in their wake. It's tracking murdering bastards and burying the dead they leave behind. It's—"

"Stop." Her shaking fingers pressed against his mouth. "I'm sorry."

This life, it hadn't been his choice. To walk alone, no, he'd never wanted that.

To kill forever.

And live in the darkness.

Torture.

All of it was hell, for him.

"I'm sorry," she whispered, and her fingers slid down to cup his jaw. Serena rose on her tiptoes. She pressed her mouth against his.

His arms locked around her as Luis pulled her tightly against him. The kiss wasn't wild this time. Not desperate.

Softer. Sweeter.

Almost...tender.

He tasted her slowly. Savored the flavor of her on his tongue. He brushed his lips over hers, so lightly. *I will never forget you, Serena. I can't. You will be what gets me through the darkness.*

After a time, Luis forced his head to lift. He considered the words she'd given to him. Serena hadn't expected to care. Well, in such a short time, he sure as hell hadn't, either. But he cared for her. He exhaled heavily. Why lie to himself? The feelings were a lot more than just mere caring.

Lust. Need. Want. Yes, he felt all of those things.

He also wanted simply to hold her. To watch her paint in the sunlight. To see her smile. To savor her as the years rolled by and time passed.

That wouldn't happen. That *couldn't* happen. It wasn't what fate had planned.

At the beginning, he'd thought he'd try to take her. To force her into his world so that he could have a bit of the burning light that he saw shining so brightly within her. But he couldn't do that. He couldn't force Serena to come into his world. Not when she didn't belong in his life of violence and death.

She needed life and passion.

She didn't need him. Even if she had started to…care for him.

His mother had warned him of this. Warned that the men in his family fell too quickly. That they could need and want too much.

His father, for all his power, had died of a broken heart. After all, no mortal weapons could kill a being like him. But the death of his beloved wife? Yes, that had done it.

Luis gazed down at his sweet witch. "Tomorrow is Halloween." A day normally celebrated by witches. All Hallows' Eve.

She gave a quick nod.

"We have to stop him before midnight. He'll bind you today if he can, and he'll try to kill you —"

"On Halloween," she finished, her voice quiet. "That's what he did to the witches in LA. Binding, then death."

Because the magic was always stronger on All Hallows' Eve. He stroked her cheek. Brushed back a stray curl. "I'm not going to let that happen."

That pert chin of hers lifted once more. "Neither am I."

Once the warlock was killed, it would be the end for them, though. Serena couldn't go with Luis where he had to travel. She couldn't, wouldn't want to spend the years of her life battling the dregs of the Other world.

The foolish plan he'd hatched in the heat of his hunger and selfish lust felt hollow now. He'd just been alone for so long, and Serena...she made him feel so alive.

Yet she deserved peace. Happiness. A happy ending, those endings that princesses got in fairy tales, but witches never did.

He'd always hated those stories. Why couldn't a witch get a happy ending?

"Are you ready?" He sure as hell wasn't.

"Yes."

Then it was time. "Let's go take down a warlock."

***

Serena drove to Roswell. She knew the area in the northern section of Atlanta well. There was no traffic on the streets. She and Luis didn't talk as they drove. Luis was tense and silent, and after her stupid confession fiasco, she wasn't about to open her mouth.

Once they reached Roswell, there were several houses that sported the white columns Jack had mentioned, but only one home was concealed behind a huge, wrought-iron gate.

"He's going to sense us," she warned, but knew Luis must have already realized that fact. She braked a distance from the big house. She didn't feel the pull of the warlock's power, not yet, but if she got much closer...

"Won't do him any good." Luis didn't sound concerned. Typical for him. "A thirty-second warning isn't going to save his ass."

No, it wouldn't. Not from Luis. And not from her.

"You don't have to come inside, Serena. Let me finish this. There's no need for you to see—"

Me kill. He didn't finish the sentence, but Serena knew exactly what Luis meant. Her spine straightened as she leveled her gaze on him. "I'm coming."

His lips parted as if he would speak, but then he merely gave a hard nod.

"Luis…" She touched his arm. "I'm not afraid to see you kill. The idea that psychotic bastards are out there and that they might get to keep hurting and killing—just like this prick has done—that frightens me."

His head cocked to the left side.

"When I saw you kill, yes, for a moment, I was afraid. But I was a whole lot more terrified when I realized just what old Jack was capable of doing—and what he'd already done." His eyes were so very golden. She loved his eyes, even when they flooded black with his demon power. Serena licked her lower lip. "Someone has to stop the darkness, and I think we're all lucky that someone is you."

"I can't stop it all. I never can."

Of course not, he was one being. And the world was so very big. And so very bad. "You make a difference, Luis. To me, to others out there, you make a huge difference. I want you to know that and to know that I won't be forgetting you, either." *I will always remember you.*

He bent his head. Brushed his lips over hers. "You damn well better not or I might just have to come back and remind you of exactly who I am."

She smiled at him.

His gaze dropped to her mouth. "You have the most beautiful smile. It's a gift I will treasure."

Had her big, bad soul hunter just called her smile a gift? That was…poetic. Sweet. Her chest burned. Before she could say anything else to him, Luis climbed from the car and shut the door.

This is it. The end. Serena inhaled slowly before she turned to push open her own door. As she stood, she realized that she didn't want Luis to leave. She didn't want him to vanish from her life as quickly as he'd come. She'd just found him. Just started to truly understand him. There was so much more that she wanted to do with Luis—

Not enough time.

Serena wasn't sure if a lifetime with Luis would be long enough.

But he was already hunting. This wasn't the time for some big, heart-felt talk. *Stop the warlock. End the nightmare.* Then maybe she and Luis could have more time.

She began stalking toward the house. She felt the stir in the air that told her one of her kind was close. One of her kind—one that had chosen the dark magic. So tempting, that magic. Offering untold power and, according to some, eternal life.

"I've got him," she whispered.

Luis gave a slight inclination of his head. "So do I."

Almost in unison, they began running forward. If they sensed the warlock, then he would have to sense them, too. His warning.

They bounded up the wooden steps of the porch. Luis blasted open the door with a wave of his hand. Serena darted after him. She was more than ready to face the bastard who had tormented her. She wanted to find him and—

A sudden, fiery pain knocked her off her feet. She fell onto the gleaming floor of the foyer as a sharp cry tore from her.

The burning cut into her muscles, dug down to the bone, and she didn't need to yank away the sleeve of her sweater to know what had happened.

The third binding mark branded her upper arm.

Bastard.

Oh, yes, she had him.

But the asshole sure had her, too.

CHAPTER THIRTEEN

Serena's cry iced his veins. Luis glanced back and saw her stumble to the floor. He reached for her—

"No!" Her face whipped up toward him. Tears slid down her cheeks. "It's the third bind—go! Stop him!"

He didn't want to leave her on the floor, crying in pain, but there was no choice. *Fucking hell.* With a last glance, he spun on his heel and stormed through the house. He could feel the magical pull of the warlock's power. There, up ahead, to the right—

A wave of his fingers sent the door flying inward. It smashed into the wall and only missed the warlock's blond head by about a foot.

Lucky bastard.

Well, not for long.

The warlock spun around. He had a small cloth and a black-hilted athame clutched in his hands. He looked at Luis for a moment, then he smiled.

Luis hesitated. A smile was not the usual way death was greeted.

"Where's the little witch?" the warlock drawled, and the knife slashed across the cloth. It cut the fabric into two pieces that fluttered to the floor.

Serena's shirt. It looked just like one he'd glimpsed in her closet. "You're not going to get her power."

The warlock's smile widened. "I've already gotten the witch's power. It's all tied up and waiting for me."

Bound.

Luis stepped forward and tried to block the image of Serena crying out in pain. His legs were braced apart, and he lifted his hands as he let his claws out. "You're going to die here, warlock."

"Michael. Michael Deveaux." The warlock shook his head. "Really, if you're going to hunt, you should at least know the name of the one you seek."

The name was familiar. A Deveaux had attacked a coven of witches back in the 1900s in South Carolina, but word had passed that he'd died in the fire that consumed the coven house and—

The warlock laughed. "Trying to figure it all out, are you, soul hunter?" He shook his head. "Come now, surely you didn't think that one of my kind wouldn't find the secret to immortality, too? Why let the vampires and your sick lot have all the fun?"

Hell.

"Most witches and wizards—those fucking idiots—think the dark path just brings pain. Terror. Death. But they're wrong. The dark can bring life, and the secret to living forever, it's so simple, really." Michael tossed the knife in his hand. The blade glinted. "All you have to do is steal a bit of magic..." His hand moved in a deceptively slow twist, and then the blade was tumbling end over end as it flew toward Luis.

What the hell? Luis knocked the knife away with a toss of his right hand. The blade clattered to the floor a few feet away. "I'm not one of your bound witches, dumbass. It'll take a whole lot more than you've got to stop me." He didn't care how old the guy was. Or how powerful the SOB thought he was. Michael Deveaux would die soon.

"I'm stronger than you think," Michael growled. "And I know what makes you weak."

A scream echoed through the house.

Serena's scream.

Michael lifted his hand—and Serena flew into the room. She was fighting desperately. Struggling against an invisible force that pulled her through the air.

Luis lunged across the room. He caught the warlock in a fierce grip and threw him against the wall.

Serena's body dropped to the floor. She scrambled across the hard wood and—

The warlock slammed his fist into Luis's chest. The full wrath of his magic was behind the blow. This time, Luis was the one who rocked back. He stumbled and slammed into the side of a chair.

Okay, so the bastard was strong.

He wasn't strong enough.

"To me, witch!" the warlock yelled. His hands lifted as power whipped through the room. Wind howled inside the house.

Serena seemed to rocket to the bastard. Michael smiled his sick, twisted grin as she screamed and shot toward him.

Luis leapt to his feet and—

Serena whipped the warlock's knife from behind her back.

Such a sneaky, clever, beautiful witch.

"Here I am, jackass!" She plunged the blade into Michael's chest.

The warlock let loose an earsplitting cry of pain and fury.

Luis caught Serena's wrist and yanked her behind him. As fast as he could, Luis threw up a spell to shield her. The warlock wouldn't touch her again—not with magic or hands.

Michael pulled the knife from his chest. "You've desecrated my athame, bitch!"

Serena gave a ragged laugh from behind Luis. "Like I give a damn! You've desecrated all of our kind!"

Enough talk. Luis grabbed the warlock. Lifted him into the air. "Tell me, Michael, have you killed witches? Bound them? Stolen their powers and their lives?" The question of guilt or innocence was always asked before death. Though Luis knew what answer he'd get from the warlock straining in his grasp.

"Yes, yes, soul hunter, I have, and I'll do it again! I'll kill those bitches and —"

Truth.

"Get ready to burn," Luis warned. The hot breath of his power flowed through him. His hands heated. The magic boiled beneath his touch and —

"You get ready," Michael snarled back and slammed his forehead into Luis's.

Luis growled at the snap of pain, but never released his hold on the warlock. The fire of his magic burned brighter. His hands began to glow.

"I'm not some weak demon, soul hunter! I'm the strongest warlock who has ever walked this earth! You won't kill me. You can't —"

A gust of wind sent the pictures flying from the walls and slid the furniture across the room.

Then the warlock managed to snatch his right hand free of Luis's grasp. His fingers went for Luis's eyes.

"Let's see what you fear, soul hunter!"

The dark spell came at Luis. Hard, fast, and too powerful to block.

His mother. Burning. Screaming his name.

His father. Lost. Dying.

Serena. Three raised slashes near her shoulder. She lay curled on the floor. Fire raced toward her. *"Luis! Help me! Luis!"*

"Dream to reality…" The warlock said as his fingers fell away. With a snap of sound, fire sparked near the curtains behind them. Then greedily swept across the room.

"Witches burn so quickly," Michael added with a cold smile. "They're so weak…"

"No!" Serena's voice. But not afraid. Furious. "Don't let him trick you!" Her fingers dug into Luis's arm. The nails he loved bit into his flesh. "Forget the flames—fight him!"

But the fire burned so hot.

I don't want to be weak. Serena's words to him.

She would never be weak.

"Luis, forget about me. He can't be allowed to hurt the coven. We have to stop him!"

Never weak. Not his Serena.

The fire was too close.

He gathered his magic and then he let the power take over. His hands burned through the warlock's clothes. Michael whimpered. Cried out in denial. Fear.

Michael's eyes widened when his magic was bound.

The fire around them faded into weak tendrils of smoke.

And when death whispered in his ear, terror twisted Michael's face as he tried to scream.

Luis pressed all the harder onto him. He felt the surge of all the dark power trapped within the warlock's body. Power that would be his. Every last bloodstained drop.

Michael began to shudder against him. Spittle flew from his mouth and the warlock choked as he tried to suck in desperate breaths. *There will be no more breath for you.*

His death was too easy. For the crimes he'd committed, he should have suffered and writhed in agony.

But that wasn't the way of the soul hunter. No, it was for another far stronger than he to give final punishment.

Luis lifted his hands.

Michael fell to the floor. The warlock's body was hard as a rock. His breath gone. His heart forever still.

Luis spun to face Serena. She was staring, lips parted, at the warlock. Luis grabbed the sleeve of her sweater and tore the fabric as he yanked it up to see her upper arm—

"What are you doing—"

Three slashes lined her upper arm. Red, angry and—

Fading. As he watched, the binding marks lightened. The raised skin lowered.

"You did it," she whispered.

He touched her soft skin. Carefully smoothed his fingers over her arm. The marks vanished completely.

Her smile was so beautiful it broke the heart he'd long forgotten. Luis swallowed once. Twice. Then finally managed to say, "You're safe, Serena, and your coven's safe."

She had her magic and her sisters of the blood. Her life would be just fine. As for his…

It would never be the same.

***

He wasn't the type for good-byes. Especially not with her.

They went back to her home and crossed the threshold just as the first rays of the dawn light trickled across the sky.

He knew that he should leave her. Just walk away.

But he couldn't, not without having her just one more time. A final time.

Luis carried Serena to her bedroom. He didn't bother turning on any of the lights. He undressed her slowly, tenderly. Kissed the hollow of her throat. Tasted the sweetness of her nipples.

His tongue laved the soft curve of her belly and teased the piercing that drove him wild.

His fingers caressed her hips. Parted her thighs. Touched the sweet heaven that waited for him.

Before, he'd known heat and wild passion with her. This time, it was different.

When he sank into her, the first thrust was slow. Her sex took him eagerly, squeezing his cock and coating him with her slick heat. Her eyes were open and locked with his as he withdrew, then thrust back into her. The rhythm was slow, but the hunger burned just as fiercely as before in his blood.

Their lips met in a kiss. Mouths open, tongues tangling. His fingers caressed the center of her arousal even as he drove into her. The bed squeaked beneath them. The scent of sex filled the air, and her taste flowed onto his tongue.

His head lifted. He raised his body, bracing his weight on his arms, and watched as his cock plunged into her.

Her pale thighs trembled.

He withdrew. Drove back into her snug sex.

Over and over. I could fuck her forever.

She came, clenching around him, and breathing out his name.

Another thrust. Another slow, deep drive into her body.

It would never be this good again. Never. No one would ever replace Serena. His witch. She'd summoned him. He'd fallen for her.

When he climaxed, he didn't call out her name.

But his soul did.

CHAPTER FOURTEEN

He was gone.

Serena knew that Luis had left her even before she opened her eyes. There was a coldness, an emptiness, in the room. In the bed.

Steeling herself, she opened her eyes. The bright light of the afternoon sun filled the room. The imprint of Luis's head was still on the nearby pillow, but he was gone.

A long-stemmed red rose lay in his place.

She reached for the flower and lifted it to her nose. The soft petals brushed against her skin. Such a sweet smell.

Such a fucking painful good-bye.

He did his job. He saved you. The coven. He had to go back to his life.

Her fingers clenched around the rose. A thorn pierced her thumb and drew blood.

He hadn't even said good-bye. Hadn't even asked if she might want him to stay…or if she might want to go with him.

"Because he's a damn soul hunter," she muttered. Serena dropped the rose back onto the pillow and glared at the flower. It was either glare or cry, and she was not going to cry. "He has to fight for the world. He doesn't have time to spend his days with a witch." But she would have liked to have spent her days and nights with him.

She hadn't bargained on needing him so much. On...loving him.

Not for a second.

He wasn't supposed to be a man that she could love. He was supposed to have been the worst kind of monster. Not the perfect mate.

She inhaled and pulled in the scent of the rose, of sex, and...of him. "No." Serena shook her head. No, she'd just been through hell. She wasn't going to skulk away now and let her dreams die. Because she'd realized when that third binding mark bit into her skin that she did have dreams. Dreams of a home. Of a man who loved her.

Dreams of Luis.

Too late. She should have told him how she felt, not that crap about *caring*, but how she really felt.

There had to be a way. Something she could do.

She'd fought the warlock.

She was sure as all hell going to fight for love.

What could she do —

Her mother's voice seemed to whisper in her ear, "The soul hunter, he comes after witches when they're bad."

A smile twisted her lips as inspiration filled her. "Time to get bad."

***

Midnight. The witching hour, as some called it.

The perfect time for her.

Serena pulled out her athame and carefully cast a circle in the dirt. A small tremble shook her hand as she gripped the knife because she couldn't help but remember the last time she'd held such a weapon. The very *recent* time.

But the athame—it shouldn't have been a weapon. It was meant for magic, not pain and death.

There had been no choice. She'd had to use the knife against Michael. She'd grabbed it when he hadn't been looking. When he'd pulled her toward him with his power, she'd attacked.

Serena exhaled and then bent to light her candles. The wind was still this night. No leaves fluttered in the breeze. As if the air itself were waiting...

Just as she had waited. Too many hours. "I summoned you once," she murmured, "and I'll do it again." The circle was cast. The words of the spell poured from her. Magic blazed in her heart.

***

Luis gazed down into his tequila and realized that if he tried hard enough, he could see Serena's reflection in the gleaming liquid.

His beautiful witch.

He'd kissed her before he left. Pressed a soft kiss to her cheek and conjured her a rose. Leaving without a word had seemed to be the right choice. Because if he'd stayed and seen her when she woke, he would have broken down...and begged her to stay with him. Not for a few days. Forever.

Forever was a very, very long time for him.

Behind him, two coyote shifters snarled as they leaned over a pool table. He didn't spare them a glance. He was far too focused on memories of his witch.

Would she have considered staying with him? Tying her soul to his so that she could share his life?

No.

Shit. Had he really been arrogant enough to think that he could claim her? Back at the beginning, for a wild moment, he had. He'd taken one look at her, fallen as hard and fast as his father had for his mother all those centuries before, and he'd thought, simply —

Mine.

But no matter how much he craved Serena, he couldn't force her into his world.

He brought the glass to his lips. Drained the fiery liquid in one swallow.

A soul bond with someone like him — that was no easy undertaking. Serena would have been forced to give up her home. Her coven. His precious witch deserved happiness, and she wouldn't find that battling demons each day of her life.

She deserved more. So much more.

So he'd given her the only gift that he could. He'd walked away to let her live a real life with someone else.

Some utterly lucky asshole who would never, ever deserve her and—

The air began to swirl around him. A small tornado that separated him from the others. Luis stilled. This had happened before. Actually, this had happened to him the first night he'd met Serena. The small tornado had appeared just seconds before Serena had—

He disappeared and his empty glass fell to the floor. The glass shattered.

***

He didn't look pissed.

Serena slowly lowered her arms and peered at Luis's face. Such a handsome face, really. Not hard at all. Strong. Determined.

Perfect.

His eyes narrowed. He stepped out of her circle. "You can't keep playing with dark magic."

"I'm not playing." The dangerous whispers in her mind as she'd performed the spell had been louder this time, but she hadn't been the least bit tempted by their lures.

She'd done the spell for one reason. Love. The dark powers in this world — and the next — couldn't touch that.

"Why, Serena?" His voice was stark. "Why risk the danger?"

"Why did you leave me without a good-bye?" The rose he'd left was on the ground near his foot. Another part of her spell.

"To spare you." Luis lifted his right hand, and she saw his claws. When he raised his left hand, she saw a ball of flames dance over his palm. "Tell me, did you truly want to wake to this in your bed every morning?"

No hesitation. Besides, she now understood that he'd know when she lied. "Yes."

His nostrils flared.

"That was a truth, wasn't it, soul hunter?"

His head jerked.

"Want to hear a few more truths from me?"

He didn't move.

Serena took his silence and stillness as a big, old yes. "I didn't expect you — oh, I knew I was getting the big, bad soul hunter, but I didn't expect *you*. You touched me, and I hungered. You stood close to me, and I felt stronger. You held me — " She was absolutely stripping her pride bare before him, but she wasn't letting him go without a fight. "And I wanted to stay in your arms forever."

Truth. She saw the knowledge in his eyes.

"I told you I cared, and that wasn't true. Or at least, it wasn't the full truth." It was so easy to see the lies and half-truths she'd told herself now. Waking up alone with hope gone had a tendency to make things crystal clear for a witch.

Or any woman.

"My body aches for you and so does my heart." Every moment that he'd been gone, her heart had hurt. She'd missed him so much. "I feel like I've been waiting for you to come into my life for years, and I didn't even know it until I woke up without you." She sounded sappy, and she wasn't the sappy type. She was the desperate type. The determined type. "If you don't want me, tell me. I'm a big girl. I can take it." Yes, it would hurt like hell, but she wouldn't stop him from leaving her. "Do not just walk away, though, without telling me good-bye. Give me that much at least and—"

And Luis had her in his arms, his hold too tight. "I can't walk away again. I won't."

Truth. Even she could sense that.

"I need you, Serena. More than I need the night. More than breath. More than magic."

Oh, hell, her knees had gone weak. He needed her more than magic?

"I left you once, and I only did it because I didn't want to force you into my world." He drew in a ragged breath. "Because if I think you're mine, if I claim you and cross that line, I'll never let you go and—"

"I am yours." Her mother had told her once that souls recognized their mates. Luis was the mate for her soul. "I've been from the beginning." Understanding that fully had just taken some time.

"If I bind us together," he rasped, "there will be no going back, don't you see that? I'll lock you to me, forever. Chain your soul to mine—"

"Oh, Luis, it already is linked." That wrenching emptiness she'd felt upon waking— her soul had missed his.

But no more. The binding he spoke of—it wasn't something she feared. No loss of powers, only a joining of spirits. "Tell me, Luis, tell me how you feel—"

"I feel like you're my world. My damn world."

She didn't try to stop the smile that stretched across her face. "Then I think you're going to be stuck with me."

"Sweetheart, forever is a very long time for me—for us—if I bind our souls, your life span will be increased to match mine—"

"Good." She'd never sought immortality, but the idea of living endless days and nights with him? Yes, she'd take it. Over and over again. "I am not afraid of what might come. I will fight by your side. Love by your side. My magic's back and I can help you. We can make this world better—"

"You already have made it better." He kissed her, and the touch of his lips so tender that she nearly cried out. "You already have made *my* life better, Serena. You make my world better just by being in it."

That was so sweet. Who would have thought...a soul hunter could say the sweetest things...

Air swirled around them. Magic warmed the night.

This was it. What she'd wanted. "Luis?"

He pressed a careful kiss to her lips. "Hold onto me. This ride might get rough."

She laughed and held on tighter. "Just the kind of ride that I like."

He kissed her again and the power bloomed between them. Serena realized that her mother had been right about so many things. If only Serena had gotten the chance to tell her so.

Souls did touch others in this world. They looked for their mates. The big, bad monsters that waited in the dark — they did come after the bad witches.

And sometimes, well, sometimes, it was good to be a little bit bad...And under love's sweet and sexy spell.

THE END

A NOTE FROM THE AUTHOR

Thank you so much for taking the time to read PUT A SPELL ON ME!

PUT A SPELL ON ME was originally released in September 2008 as part of the EVERLASTING BAD BOYS anthology (back then, the novella had the title of SPELLBOUND). I revised and updated the story, and I was happy to send my soul hunter back into the world. I hope that you enjoyed his adventures, and there will be more of my "classic" paranormals being re-released very soon. So prepare for more stories in the "Other" world.

If you'd like to stay updated on my releases and sales, please join my newsletter list.

https://cynthiaeden.com/newsletter/

Again, thank you for reading PUT A SPELL ON ME.

Best,
Cynthia Eden
cynthiaeden.com

ABOUT THE AUTHOR

Cynthia Eden is a *New York Times*, *USA Today*, *Digital Book World*, and *IndieReader* best-seller.

Cynthia writes sexy tales of contemporary romance, romantic suspense, and paranormal romance. Since she began writing full-time in 2005, Cynthia has written over one hundred novels and novellas.

Cynthia lives along the Alabama Gulf Coast. She loves romance novels, horror movies, and chocolate.

For More Information
- *https://cynthiaeden.com*
- *http://www.facebook.com/cynthiaedenfanpage*

HER OTHER WORKS

Wilde Ways

- Protecting Piper (Book 1)
- Guarding Gwen (Book 2)
- Before Ben (Book 3)
- The Heart You Break (Book 4)
- Fighting For Her (Book 5)
- Ghost Of A Chance (Book 6)
- Crossing The Line (Book 7)
- Counting On Cole (Book 8)
- Chase After Me (Book 9)
- Say I Do (Book 10)

Dark Sins

- Don't Trust A Killer (Book 1)
- Don't Love A Liar (Book 2)

Lazarus Rising

- Never Let Go (Book One)
- Keep Me Close (Book Two)
- Stay With Me (Book Three)
- Run To Me (Book Four)
- Lie Close To Me (Book Five)
- Hold On Tight (Book Six)

- Lazarus Rising Volume One (Books 1 to 3)
- Lazarus Rising Volume Two (Books 4 to 6)

Dark Obsession Series

- Watch Me (Book 1)
- Want Me (Book 2)
- Need Me (Book 3)
- Beware Of Me (Book 4)
- Only For Me (Books 1 to 4)

Mine Series

- Mine To Take (Book 1)
- Mine To Keep (Book 2)
- Mine To Hold (Book 3)
- Mine To Crave (Book 4)
- Mine To Have (Book 5)
- Mine To Protect (Book 6)
- Mine Box Set Volume 1 (Books 1-3)
- Mine Box Set Volume 2 (Books 4-6)

Bad Things

- The Devil In Disguise (Book 1)
- On The Prowl (Book 2)
- Undead Or Alive (Book 3)
- Broken Angel (Book 4)
- Heart Of Stone (Book 5)
- Tempted By Fate (Book 6)
- Wicked And Wild (Book 7)
- Saint Or Sinner (Book 8)
- Bad Things Volume One (Books 1 to 3)

- Bad Things Volume Two (Books 4 to 6)
- Bad Things Deluxe Box Set (Books 1 to 6)

Bite Series

- Forbidden Bite (Bite Book 1)
- Mating Bite (Bite Book 2)

Blood and Moonlight Series

- Bite The Dust (Book 1)
- Better Off Undead (Book 2)
- Bitter Blood (Book 3)
- Blood and Moonlight (The Complete Series)

Purgatory Series

- The Wolf Within (Book 1)
- Marked By The Vampire (Book 2)
- Charming The Beast (Book 3)
- Deal with the Devil (Book 4)
- The Beasts Inside (Books 1 to 4)

Bound Series

- Bound By Blood (Book 1)
- Bound In Darkness (Book 2)
- Bound In Sin (Book 3)
- Bound By The Night (Book 4)
- Bound in Death (Book 5)
- Forever Bound (Books 1 to 4)

Other Romantic Suspense

- One Hot Holiday

- Secret Admirer
- First Taste of Darkness
- Sinful Secrets
- Until Death
- Christmas With A Spy